*a* **DOG** **RL**

**MYSTERIES**

**2**

*Dead Man's*

**BEST FRIEND**

# a DOG and his GIRL MYSTERIES

## 2

## Dead Man's BEST FRIEND

### Jane B. Mason
### and Sarah Hines Stephens

SCHOLASTIC INC.

ISBN 978-0-545-43625-0

12 11 10 9 8 7 6 5 4 3 2      14 15 16 17/0

Printed in the U.S.A.    40
First printing, June 2013

The text type was set in Adobe Garamond Pro.
Book design by Nina Goffi

# CHAPTER 1

By the time I figured out what was happening, it was too late. The crime had been committed and the perp had escaped. On *my* watch. *Woof.*

It was a hard, cold fact that K-9s lost criminals from time to time. Even well-trained ones like me. Still, it was enough to make my ears lay flat.

The problem? My senses were working overtime.

I had one eye on my girl, Cassie, and her friend Taylor, the cool kid from Pet Rescue. They were working to bring in strays. I had one ear on the puppy in the crate next to me — the dog Taylor had already caught and was calling

Daisy. The little pit bull smelled nothing like a flower. She smelled like motor oil and garbage and neglect.

My nose was ignoring Daisy's stink and inhaling the smoky, juicy, beefy smell of Smokehouse burgers. Burgers Cassie and Taylor were using to bait the strays. Burgers still hot from the Smokehouse. Dripping with meaty goodness. Sitting in a bag right next to me.

I might have been drooling. I might have been a little distracted. But that was no excuse.

I was on the job, on a Sit Stay. Just far enough away from the desperate dogs we were trying to capture not to scare them. Just close enough to the loading dock to watch for quivering noses. I was watching and waiting and smelling and staring. And yes, drooling and dreaming of leftovers.

That was how the perp pulled off the burger heist. And he never would have gotten away if the bag had been on my good side — the side with the ear that still worked. I knew better than to keep precious goods on my bad side. But even a dog can make mistakes.

When I heard the crinkle I whipped my head around.

Fast. Only not fast enough. The dog was gone. And so was the bag of delicious. We'd been burger burgled!

There was no point in barking out the alarm for Cassie and Taylor. The four-footed thief had already hightailed it out of there. And like I said, I was on a Sit Stay. A dog like me knows that a Sit Stay also means "quiet." Civilian dogs didn't understand the importance of a good command. A well-trained K-9 did. I was well trained.

Also, barking would have scared the street meats. A big, loud bark could send the homeless pups running far and fast. A dog didn't have to be on the streets for long to learn. Out here everyone and everydog was against him. Every meal could be his last. Just the mood down here on the waterfront was making me feel a little rattled. A little worried about losing my soft bed. My bowl. My Bunny.

I was glad when Taylor tapped Cassie's shoe. "It's getting late," he said. "I think we'd better call it." The day was darkening.

Cassie stood up and brushed herself off. She looked droopy-eared. She was a girl who liked to get her dog, and she was good at it. But today she'd come up empty-handed.

I wagged, and she almost smiled. Then she noticed the missing burger bag. I stopped wagging. Her eyes asked me a question, and my eyes answered. Sometimes that was all Cassie and I needed: eyes. She knew I hadn't eaten the bait, but Taylor was suspicious.

"Dodge, you devil," he scolded playfully.

I let out a bark to tell him I was innocent, but he was already getting on his bike. He waved good-bye and headed out, pulling a little trailer with Daisy's kennel behind. The pit bull was still shaking in her crate, but was going to Pet Rescue, the shelter where Taylor worked and Cassie volunteered. She'd get a bath, a real dinner, and a warm place to sleep. She didn't know it yet, but she was on the road to home. Maybe even a forever-home.

Cassie pushed her bike into a roll before swinging her leg over the seat. I was right with her, ready to go. She pedaled fast and I broke into a run, feeling the wind in my ears and fur and nose. I let my tongue loll out of my mouth, just a little. I tasted the air. It felt good to run, to be on the move. To be running away from the warehouses. This neighborhood was no friend to dogs.

I had a great pace going when Cassie squeezed her brakes. I slowed, smelling warm rubber and something else. We were still near the water. I sniffed. Seaweed. Gasoline. Vegetables?

I followed Cassie's gaze to see why we'd stopped. She was staring at two men outside a vegetable-scented warehouse. They were shouting and posing like circling dogs.

One of the men had on a white apron. He puffed his chest and stuck out his chin as he howled out angry words. The other man wore a coat and the kind of special collar men wear around their necks to look fancy. Only the cloth seemed to be choking him — his face was all swollen. The shiny car behind him matched his shoes. It had to be his. And next to the car was an even larger man who was hiding his face under a hat.

I stifled the growl in my throat. I smelled lies. Or maybe horseradish.

The man in the collar put his hand on the apron man's shoulder. It might have seemed easygoing, like a pat. But it wasn't. It was more like a nip at the back of the neck. A signal to let the other guy know that he was in charge. He chuckled, but not in a friendly way. Then he took his hand off the other man, turned, and got into the shiny car. In the back, where the criminals sit. The hat guy got in front and they drove away.

Apron man watched them go. His hands were balled into fists. The tang of frustration and anger reached my nose, making me want to chase the shiny car. Maybe even bite its tires.

Cassie watched. She drummed her fingers on her handlebars as the taillights faded in the semidark. "Interesting," she said, and we pushed off.

I ran faster but didn't enjoy the run — just the idea of being home. For dinner. *Dinner, dinner, dinner.* I loved dinner. Dinner was my favorite.

When we walked in, I smelled two things: bacon frying and that something wasn't right. The Dad was in the kitchen, cooking the bacon. "Hi, guys," he greeted. But he barely looked up. Cassie hurried to set the table. I started to pant, just a little. And pace. *Click, click, click, click.* In front of the door.

Cassie put the plates out and dropped napkins on the dining table. I could tell she was feeling what I was smelling.

6

Something not right. The napkins weren't landing in their usual places. Her eyebrows were low. She wasn't smiling. Not even close. She looked out the window at the setting sun. She looked back at the clock in the kitchen. Then she looked at me, still pacing. I sat.

Cassie patted her leg and I followed her into the kitchen for kibble. But even as I crunched down my dinner, I kept my good ear cocked. Listening. Waiting to hear a car or footsteps or the phone.

The Dad was draining a pot of steaming spaghetti. He was making pasta carbonara, aka pasta deliciousness. What could be better than pasta, bacon, eggs, and cheese? The smell alone was usually enough to keep me drooling under the table. But not tonight. Tonight the smell of worry was ruining everything.

When my bowl was licked clean, I started pacing again. Back and forth. Dining room to front door. The Sister carried plates of hot pasta to the table. She practically knocked into Cassie.

"What are you doing?" Cassie barked. She and The Sister didn't always get along. "Mom's not even here yet."

The Sister didn't reply; she just stared. I stopped in my

tracks. Cassie'd said it. She'd said what the not-right feeling was about. The Mom wasn't home, and she hadn't called. It was late. Dinner was ready. And The Mom wasn't home.

Sure, sometimes The Mom worked late. She had a big job. She was the top dog — The Chief — at the Bellport Police Station, where I used to work. And she was good at it. Very good. So sometimes she stayed late. Sometimes she traveled. Sometimes she missed dinner. But she always called.

Dinner was a big deal with the Sullivan Pack. You weren't allowed to miss it without a good excuse. The whole family was trained to be home for dinner, even The Mom. Only tonight she hadn't called. That meant something was off. Way off.

"Shouldn't we wait?" Cassie asked. She gave The Sister the kind of look I generally reserve for The Cat. The girls glared at each other. It was a standoff. Neither of them looked away, even when The Brother slunk into the room and plopped down in his usual spot. There was no way I was going to sit in *my* usual spot, which was under the table. Not without The Mom here. I needed to pace.

"Dad said to go ahead and serve," The Sister snapped. She smiled with her mouth, but her eyes were growling.

"It's true, I did." The Dad ended the stare down when he set two more steamy plates on the table. He tried to sound calm but looked twitchy. Tired. He didn't have much fur on his head, and what was left was sticking straight up. He'd been running his fingers through it. The way some dogs lick themselves hairless when they get anxious. "We can't wait any longer. Carbonara's only good when it's hot." His shoulders went up and down.

I'd heard The Dad say this before. Carbonara was his specialty. He liked to howl about the "beauty" and "economy" of using the heat of boiled pasta to cook the eggs. I had no idea what any of that meant. I just loved carbonara. So did the rest of the Sullivan Pack. The only dependable leftovers on carbonara night were the bits that Cassie saved for me, which were a sacrifice.

Tonight, though, there'd be plenty of leftovers. I heard forks on plates, twirling the eggy noodles. But nobody was eating.

"Maybe she just forgot to call," Cassie said. "Maybe

she's just having a bad day." My girl was always hoping for the best. Just like a dog.

"Maybe," The Dad said. "It's weird she didn't answer her cell, though. That's not like her." He ran his fingers through his hair again, then stopped. He smiled at his kids. He didn't like to bring up the dangers that came with being Chief. He thought worrying was his job, and he worried enough for the whole pack. Right now it looked like he was going to worry away what was left of his fur.

The Dad opened his mouth but stopped when lights flashed through the front window. Two lights. Headlights. The Mom was home!

I listened at the door for footsteps outside, but all I heard was a car door and the engine of a patrol car. Still running. Why was the engine running? The car door had already closed. . . .

Finally Cassie caught up to me and turned the latch. I pushed with my front feet, and swung the door wide so I could jump down the front steps. But I didn't see The Mom on the doorstep, waiting to hang up her badge for the day. No. I saw Hero — my replacement on the force. He was hanging out the front squad car window in our driveway. I wanted to whine. Or run. I braced myself instead.

Hero leaped out of the car window and bounded toward me like a rabbit. Ears straight up and mouth wide open. He was a German shepherd, like me, and had also been trained to work with police. But that was where the similarities ended. Hero was all enthusiasm, no discipline. And he was approaching at top speed.

There was no place to hide. All I could do was stand there while the green K-9 wagged and drooled all over me. He bowed, paws out, begging me to play. He clearly had no idea what it meant to be on duty. I ignored him as best I could while his officer, Hank Riley, tried to calm him down.

I focused on The Mom. She was there, pulling her stuff out of the backseat of the patrol car. Wait. The backseat! The backseat was for criminals. The Chief never rode there.

I struggled to understand what I was seeing. It was hard with Hero circling and barking at me like I was a long-lost littermate. *Oh, woof!*

"That's enough, Hero," Riley said. The guy may as well have been talking to a cat. Hero wasn't listening.

Riley yanked his leash. Finally Hero sat, whimpering and squirming. Completely pathetic.

"Thanks for the ride, Riley," The Mom said. I could hear the tired in her voice.

"Sure thing, Chief," Riley said. Only he half swallowed the word "chief" and started coughing. "Anytime," he added when he'd recovered.

The Mom raised her hand in a wave, and I walked beside her up to the stoop. The smell of worry was all over her. Stronger than bacon. Stronger than garlic. Stronger than anything. But it wasn't just worry I smelled. There was an anxiousness to it, and anger, and worse . . . defeat.

The Mom waited for her pack to clear a path, stepped inside, and dropped her bag by the door. She shrugged off her coat.

"Long day?" The Dad asked, twisting his napkin.

"You could say that." The Mom sank into her chair at the table. She stared at the bowl of pasta cooling in front of her. I wanted to tell her I'd eat it if she needed me to. She didn't look hungry. Instead I settled under the table with my head on Cassie's foot — my regular spot. The perfect place to watch and listen for fallen food and dropped clues. Only nobody was eating. And nobody was talking.

For a long while the only sound was the clink of forks pushing pasta. Finally Cassie wiggled her toes and took a deep breath. "Mom, is everything okay? What's going on?"

The Chief's fork clattered down. She cleared her throat and uncrossed her legs. Her hands appeared under the table, and she laid her palms flat on her thighs. "I've been suspended from the force," she announced. "Until further notice."

# CHAPTER 2

I stared at my plate and wished I could eat. I wished I wanted even a single bite. But right now my head was so full of jumbled thoughts that my stomach had gone all queasy, and putting food into it would only make it worse.

Mom. Suspended. It just didn't make any sense. Mom was the chief of the Bellport Police Department. She had a flawless record. She was well respected, and well liked — a top-notch cop. She'd never do anything that might get her suspended.

"So what happened?" Dad asked, setting down his fork.

"What'd you do?" my older brother, Owen, piled on.

Mom sighed. "I didn't *do* anything. But I've been accused of negligence, so they're placing me on suspension while they complete the investigation."

Negligence? Mom? She was the queen of the *i* dotters and *t* crossers, Captain Careful, the Ruler of Rules.

"So this is standard procedure?" Dad asked, fishing. "Just a simple investigation?" His fingers were laced together over his plate of uneaten food.

I turned to Mom, who was looking more and more like a melting snowman. "I'm afraid it's not standard or simple," she said. "They're looking into the warehouse explosions. They're investigating Mark's death and trying to nail the responsible party."

When I heard Uncle Mark's name, I felt like the air was sucked out of the room — like we were in the cabin of an airplane and somebody opened the door. The five of us just sat there gasping. Dodge's head grew heavier on my foot, and I struggled to digest what I'd just heard. Mom was being accused of killing Uncle Mark — Dad's brother, Dodge's police partner, Mom's right hand on the force, and the best uncle anybody'd ever had.

When Uncle Mark died in the warehouse fire over a year ago, it left a huge hole in our lives — one that would never be filled. It took us a long time to recover from the shock and the loss, and even now it could suddenly feel as fresh and as painful as it did when it happened.

I stared down at my pasta, at the pieces of crispy bacon and flecks of chopped parsley. The room was deathly silent and I wanted to throw up. My hand fell under the table. Dodge sat up and I caressed the spot behind his black ears. I knew he'd been listening to every word. He wasn't shaking, but his muscles were tensed and he jumped at the sound of Mom's chair legs scraping across the floor.

I hoped Mom was standing up to say something else, to tell us what her plan was, that everything was going to be all right.

All she did was pick up her plate. "I guess I don't have much appetite," she said quietly, apologizing. "I'll be on cleanup."

"No, Mom. I'll do it," Sam piped up. "It's my night."

My head whipped around, and Dodge crawled out from under the table. We couldn't believe our ears. My ten-year-old sister was many things, but worker bee was not one of them. She usually only jumped at the chance to get *out* of a chore.

Mom held firm. "That's okay, Sammy," she said, putting a hand on my sister's shoulder. "I want to do it. It'll help me focus."

Sam eyed Mom's hand, clearly wishing she would focus on explaining how she was going to make everything better. I could relate.

I picked up my plate, too. "Sam and I will clear for you," I said, feeling hopeful. Maybe a sink of suds would help Mom develop a plan of attack, and if Sam and I stuck close by we'd be there to hear it. "No objections, Chief!" I added a little too enthusiastically. Owen peered at me through his shaggy bangs with a look that said, "Chief? Really?"

He was right. Mom's face wilted when she heard her stripped job title. Her stressed look slumped into a depressed look, and I wished I could yank the words back.

"Yeah, we'll clear," Sam chirped, trying to save the moment. She got up and took Mom's plate. Mom forced a smile and held up her hands in mock surrender, but her skin was creased between her eyebrows and her lips formed a straight line. Feeling guilty, I helped Sam carry everything into the kitchen.

Well, almost everything. When nobody was looking I put my full plate on the floor for Dodge. He looked at me unenthusiastically before digging in. I'm pretty sure he was only eating it so he wouldn't hurt my feelings. Owen put his plate down for Dodge, too, then retreated to his basement hideaway. Dodge barely even sniffed his second course.

"Oh, Dodge," I sighed as we headed up to our room. "I think this is going to get ugly." Dodge bounded a few steps ahead and looked back expectantly. "I know," I said. "Right now we just have to wait and see what happens."

I followed my dog down the hall and he pushed open the door to our room with his snout. I set my cell phone on my dresser. Normally, when I had big news or a problem I needed help with, I'd call my best friend, Hayley Gault. Hayley was the greatest thing on two legs. She gave excellent advice, cracked me up, and baked the most delicious brownies I'd ever tasted. But this problem didn't feel normal; it felt out of my league. My gut sensed something terrible, and my gut was usually right.

The other reason I didn't call Hayley was, well, it just didn't seem right to tell *anybody* about Mom's suspension. For one thing, I didn't have the whole story, and I knew from past experience that talking about a small part of a terrible situation could make it even more terrible. In my twelve years on the planet I'd noticed that humans had a way of assuming the worst when they let their imaginations fill in the blanks. Unlike dogs, who almost always assumed the *best*. So I decided to keep this situation between me and Dodge, at least for now.

We flopped onto our beds and I stared at the ceiling, stroking the soft fur between Dodge's shoulder blades. Dodge chewed his sleep buddy Bunny's ear, puffing air out his nose. We were anxious. We lay there together, listening to the sounds of the house.

Mom was lathering in the kitchen. Dad was holed up in the office on the computer. Sam was heading upstairs with the phone pressed to her ear. Owen was in his cave. Everybody was there, but nobody was home.

# CHAPTER 3

Most nights Cassie dozed off pretty fast. Once she fell asleep, I liked to take a little sniff and prowl around the neighborhood. But I always waited until her breathing was steady and her heartbeat slowed. Then I headed out on my nightly rounds. Tonight, though, things were off. We weren't sleeping. Cassie stared at the ceiling. I nibbled Bunny's ear. These were the things that usually helped us relax. Only neither of us was relaxing.

It took so long for Cassie to fall asleep I accidentally fell asleep first. And worse, I dreamed. Not good dreaming, like chasing rabbits or stealing The Cat's food. No. I dreamed horrible dreams. I dreamed of the time *before*.

I didn't like to think about that before time. Ever. Only sometimes, when I was asleep, parts of it came creeping back. Including the awful ending.

My paws twitched uselessly in an effort to escape the nightmare. I barked desperately but was paralyzed by sleep. My mouth and lips barely worked. Finally I barked so loudly I woke myself up.

When my eyes blinked open, I was instantly on all fours — standing on my bed with fur on end. I was ready for a fight. Too bad you can't shred a dream.

Outside Cassie's window the sky was getting light. I shook myself hard and looked again. Still light. I hadn't *just* fallen asleep, I'd slept most of the night! There was no time left for recon. Too late for rounds, and I didn't want to lie back down. I didn't want to close my eyes again. I didn't want to slide back into that terrible dream. I thought maybe downstairs, on the squishy couch, I might sleep without dreaming. Maybe I wouldn't be haunted there.

I put my face close to Cassie and felt her breathing, warm and steady. I hid Bunny under the bed and padded down to the living room. The couch sounded better with each step, but before I even got to it I realized I wasn't the only one awake.

Light and noises were coming from the office. I pushed the door with my snout, opening it just wide enough to slip through. The Mom looked up. She had circles under her eyes. "Hey, Dodge," she said. Her voice was scratchy and she looked like she hadn't slept at all.

The Mom lifted her bag and started to dig through it. "Where are those keys?" she mumbled. She put her hand on her forehead and gazed around the room. The drawers to the desk were open. The desktop was messy. She had been searching for a while. She needed a break.

"Whuff," I barked softly so I wouldn't wake anyone who'd managed to sleep. "Whuff," I barked again, loud enough to get The Mom out of the office.

"Time for breakfast, Dodge?" she asked. Her smile was weak. "It's a little early, but since we're both up . . ."

I wagged and she followed me into the kitchen. I scarfed down my chow in just a few bites while she started the coffee. Then I stationed myself by the counter where I could keep an eye on The Mom and catch the upcoming breakfast crumbs.

The Mom and I were still the only ones awake when her cell phone rang in her bathrobe pocket.

"Hello?" she answered.

The phone buzzed.

"Mayor Baudry. Yes, I'm awake. I didn't expect to hear back from you so soon."

Baudry. My tail thumped in recognition. I knew that guy. But The Mom was talking to him in her chirpy voice — a voice she didn't usually use with the mayor.

The phone buzzed again. It buzzed for a long time while The Mom used her thumbnail to scratch up a patch of dried milk on the counter.

I wished my good ear could understand what the insect-like noises in the phone were saying. I had no idea how people did that.

"Of course anything you can do would be great, but I don't think it's possible while I'm suspended."

Her voice was getting beggy. It made me wince.

"Yes, anything you can do. We really count on my income."

Pause.

"Thank you so much, Morris."

She hung up, shoulders sagging. I covered my nose with my paw, embarrassed for her. The Chief wasn't a groveler. Alphas don't beg . . . unless their lives depend on it.

By the time the sun came through the back windows and warmed patches on the floor, the rest of the pack was up. It was the regular rising time for them, but nothing else about it felt regular.

The Mom was still in pajamas even though she hadn't slept. Everyone noticed; it was impossible not to. The Mom was always in uniform before anyone else opened their eyes, and in running clothes before light on weekends.

"I thought I'd take a vacation day," she said lamely, pouring herself another cup of coffee. Nobody laughed. They just tried to eat their breakfasts and get out of the house as soon as they could. Cassie looked me in the eyes and told me to take care of The Mom. Then we were alone. Me. The Mom. The Cat. I thought The Mom might get dressed, but she just sat in the kitchen. She stayed. And stared. Just stayed and stared.

It was depressing to see her like that. Doing nothing. Like watching a cattle dog with no cattle to herd.

It was depressing for another reason, too. I was trapped. No sneaking out. No napping on the couch. No disciplining The Cat. Nothing but keeping an eye on The Mom and watching The Cat gloat. Depressing and humiliating.

The Cat knew she had the upper paw, too. She paraded along the back of the couch, stopping in the middle. She raised her hind leg like a flag and began to groom herself. On the couch, where I couldn't go. Cats. If she could have laughed out loud, she'd have howled.

I looked longingly at the forbidden couch cushions and flopped down on the carpet — the thin carpet on the hard floor. I put both of my paws over my nose and let out a breath. It was going to be a very long "until further notice."

# CHAPTER 4

No question about it: mopey Mom in her pajamas was totally depressing. The day after that awful dinner, I'd gotten home to find her still wearing pajamas, still looking lost and haunted. But within two days of her suspension I discovered a version of Mom that was even more alarming: Drill Sergeant Mom. One day she was drifting aimlessly around the house, and the next she was running it like she ran the police department.

"I want all of you home immediately after school today," she announced at breakfast on Thursday morning. "Operation Clean starts at four o'clock sharp!" She was dressed in an old pair of jeans and a T-shirt, but the entire outfit had been ironed, and the jeans were secured snugly around her hips with a belt.

"But I've got a big science project due on Monday," Sam said.

Mom leveled her gaze at my little sister over the rim of her coffee mug. "Then I suggest you beeline it from school," she said between sips. "The sooner you finish your cleaning duties, the sooner you can get to work on your report."

I gulped down my orange juice while Dodge scooched closer to my leg. Mom was serious; there'd be no getting out of Operation Clean.

"This is gonna suck," Owen whispered as we loaded our dishes into the dishwasher.

I nodded my agreement. "No kidding. Maybe she'll turn back into mopey Mom while we're at school."

Dodge let out a wistful sigh, and Owen ruffled his neck fur. "I feel for you, boy," he said. "Being stuck here with her all day can't be fun."

Dodge gave him a look that said "Don't remind me" and plodded into the living room to his usual spot on the floor. I grabbed my jacket and backpack and came over to give him a kiss good-bye.

"A nice long nap might help," I told him.

Dodge thumped his tail in response, and I headed out the door.

When I came back through the door seven hours later, Dodge was waiting for me, his eyebrows looking decidedly worried.

"Hey, boy," I said, dropping low for a face-to-face. Dodge licked my cheek, whimpering, and led me into the kitchen. Sam and Owen were already there, looking miserable, and it didn't take a detective to see why. The entire kitchen table was covered in cleaning supplies. Buckets, mops, rags, sponges, and cleansers of all kinds were organized in neat rows, by category. Not only was Operation Clean actually happening, The Chief had taken cleaning the house to a whole new level. "Our mission is twofold," Mom said with her hands on her hips. "To get the house in tip-top shape, and to find my missing keys."

Owen didn't seem to be listening. "What's the toothbrush for?" he asked, picking up the red plastic wand.

"For you," Mom replied with a smile. "You'll need it to get the gunk out of the grout on the kitchen floor." She handed him a bucket and a product called "Tile Sparkle." "You'd better get to it — it's a big floor."

Owen opened his mouth to protest. Then he seemed to remember that Mom had been suspended "until further notice" and that he'd better be on his best behavior — at least for now. Silently taking the bucket and the bottle, he got to work in the corner by the stove.

"Sam, you're on downstairs bathroom." Mom handed her cleanser — Toilet Bowl Bright — a sponge, and a couple of rags. "The toilet brush is in the bathroom. Make sure you scrub *behind* the toilet — it gets pretty gross back there."

"Eeewww," Sam said, pulling a face.

"Not when you're done with it," Mom said, still smiling.

Sighing heavily, my little sister took the supplies and flounced off to the bathroom.

Dodge was practically sitting on my feet, and I was grateful for his presence as I braced for my cleaning assignment. "Cassie, you're on the office. It's a mess in there, so you might have to do a little organizing along with the dusting. Those bookshelves haven't been touched in months."

*Score!* I thought as I tried to look upset. I didn't want Mom to suspect how pleased I was. Compared to the kitchen floor and the toilet, I was getting off easy. And if there was one thing I didn't mind organizing, it was Mom's files. Dodge and I could do some serious digging in there. . . .

Dodge was through the door first, sniffing his way straight to the desk, which was a disaster.

"A little organizing is right," I said.

I set the cleaning stuff on a chair and eyed the desk. Receipts, pens, papers, binder clips, newspapers, magazines, notebooks, and coffee cups were spread across the entire surface.

I dove in and began sorting things into piles. Mom had a *lot* of old papers, and even more receipts. I scanned every piece that came through my hands, trying not to let disappointment take over as the sorted stacks grew and my hopes of finding a clue shrank. There was nothing here that had anything to do with Mom's suspension or Uncle Mark — it was just endless sorting.

"Maybe the bathroom would've been a better job," I mumbled. Dodge gave me a sympathetic look, then got to his feet and stretched, a big doggy stretch with his butt in the air. Yawning, he ambled out of the room. Who could blame him? I was totally bored, too.

Sighing heavily, I dropped a handful of paper clips into the drawer and started to stack newspapers for recycling. And then I saw it, there on the bottom of the last pile. The corner of a manila folder. I pulled it out. A *thick* manila folder with the words "Corps Investigation" written on the tab. *That* was not for the general file. *That* looked intriguing.

My heart started racing. I shoved the stuff off the chair and sat down, flipping the folder open. My eyes widened as I leafed through the pages. Newspaper clippings, police documents, memos. There was a ton of stuff in here — stuff I wanted to read. I considered swiping the whole thing right then and there but knew that if Mom found out it was missing, I'd be in major trouble. Maybe I could copy a few of the documents and come back later. . . .

I grabbed three papers off the top that looked like they might be important. They were all about The Corps — a criminal ring that operated in Providence but was rumored to have its headquarters in Bellport. Keeping one eye peeled on the door, I scanned an article about a ribbon-cutting ceremony for the opening of the new community center. There was a picture of Mayor Baudry with a pair of giant scissors. The caption read: *Mayor Baudry and William Kemper proudly unveil new center.* But stuck to the article was a Post-it note with an arrow drawn on it, pointing toward another man in the crowd. It was hard to see his face because he was turned. Next to the arrow was a single word, or name, that made no sense to me at all: Slatterly. Who was Slatterly?

A whimper made me raise my head and slam the folder shut. "Dodge?" I called. The only response was the scraping of something against the floor. It sounded like the front hall bench. Peeking out the door, I spotted Dodge's behind sticking up in the air.

"Whatcha after, boy?" I put the folder back on the desk, at the bottom of the pile so I could come back to it.

In the entry hall Dodge was shoving shoes out from under the bench with his snout. He'd pushed about six pairs out when I heard the clink of keys.

Grasping Mom's keychain in his teeth, Dodge pulled them from under the seat and victoriously set them in my hand.

"We found the missing keys!" I shouted.

"Woof!" Dodge agreed triumphantly.

"Thank *God*," Sam called from her perch in front of the bathroom mirror (where she was inspecting her face for zits she'd probably never have). It looked as though she hadn't moved at all — the cleaning stuff sat untouched by the toilet. "She's been making me crazy looking for those!" Sam complained.

I shot my sister a "give me a break" look. "She's making us *all* crazy. About everything," I quietly reminded her as Mom came into the hall.

"My keys!" Mom exclaimed. "Where were they?"

"On the floor, under the coat hooks," I said, handing them over. "Dodge found them."

Mom jingled the keys lightly, looking happier than I'd seen her in days. She got down on her knees and gave Dodge a thank-you hug. "What a good boy," she praised him.

"What's so crucial about that set of keys?" I asked as Owen slouched up to us.

Mom held her just-a-sec finger in the air, pulled her phone out of her pocket, and dialed. When nobody answered, she hung up. "What was that?"

"The keys," I repeated. "Why so important?"

A shadow crossed her face, erasing any cheeriness the keys had delivered. "Apparently I wasn't supposed to bring them home," she explained, her eyebrows knitting together. "They need them at the station so they can look into my files. *Their* files, I suppose," she added with a sigh.

The word "files" buzzed in my brain and I glanced down at Dodge, an idea coming to me. "You want me to drop them off for you?" I asked, trying to sound helpful. I could get to the folder on her desk later — I doubted it was going anywhere — but the files at the station . . .

Mom sighed. She looked tired all of a sudden, probably thinking about how she wasn't allowed at the station. "That'd be great," she said. Before she could change her mind, I grabbed my backpack and sweatshirt off the hook.

Sam paused in her chin examination and came out of the bathroom looking hopeful. Since the keys had been located, maybe Operation Clean would be canceled. But before she could even open her mouth, drill sergeant Mom was leveling a finger at her. "I didn't say you were done." She stepped through the bathroom doorway and pointed. "That toilet still needs some serious scrubbing, and the sink is a disgrace. What have you been doing?"

It was a good time to make a hasty exit! I brushed past Owen on my way to the door. "Lucky," he mouthed at me.

"Jealous," I mouthed back. Not that I disagreed. I *was* lucky, and I'd be jealous, too. But hey, I thought of it first!

# CHAPTER 5

I gave an undignified yip as we headed down the driveway. I was that happy to be out of the house. All those cleaning smells made my nose twitch, in a bad way. Plus we were walking, which meant we'd be out longer. *Woof!*

I kept up easily as we turned onto the sidewalk and headed toward the center of town. Normally I didn't like to go to the station. It reminded me of the time *before*. The time I tried to forget. But I'd been cooped up all day and we were just doing a quick errand. Nothing I couldn't handle.

We headed down Kentucky Street until we got to Third, then turned toward Chestnut. Cassie pushed open the door. Deb Brubaker, the dispatcher at the front desk, greeted us with a smile.

"Hi, guys," she said, looking up from her computer monitor.

"Hey, Deb," Cassie replied, and I wagged halfheartedly. Deb was friendly enough, but I felt weird knowing The Mom was no longer welcome here. *It's temporary. Like a case of fleas*, I reminded myself. *We just need the right treatment.*

Cassie led the way into the heart of the station. A few people glanced up at us and we got more smiles. But they weren't real smiles. They were sad "sorry" smiles.

I stuck close to Cassie, licking my chops. I felt a little anxious. When Cassie visited the station in the before time, she was treated like royalty. There were doughnuts and patrol car rides, with flashing lights. My old partner would let Cassie spin in his chair until she got sick. Now I felt a little sick just thinking about my old partner. I stole a quick glance at my girl. She wasn't looking so hot herself.

I could smell sadness seeping out of her skin. Overripe berries. She was remembering my old partner, too.

When we got to The Chief's office, Chase Langtree gave us the most pathetic look of all. It was better than the fake smiles we'd gotten from the other two-leggeds, but my tail drooped anyway.

"What are you guys doing here?" Langtree asked.

Cassie held up the keys. They clinked, and my ears twitched. Both of them. Sometimes my bad ear still tried to work. "Brought these back for my mom. And she asked me to get something from her office," she added. She made it sound like nothing weird was going on. Then added, "She's really missing you guys."

My girl was playing Langtree. She was pretending not to be a threat so she'd be welcomed back into the pack. Humans did this with words. Dogs did it with whines and paced circles.

"Yeah, we miss her, too," Langtree replied with a nod.

"Do you think she'll be back soon?" Cassie asked. She was hiding her digging with innocence.

Langtree paused too long. "I hope so," he said. What he meant was "no."

Cassie sighed in disappointment but kept talking. "'Negligence' sounds so harsh, you know? Mom knows what she's doing."

Langtree looked right at her, trying to decide if he should challenge her. Trying to guess how much she knew.

"She told me all about it," Cassie assured him. I nuzzled up against my girl's leg. Even from down here I could feel her heart thundering. I smelled her nervousness. She didn't like to lie, especially about The Mom.

"It's really awful when things go that wrong," Langtree said slowly. He was looking at me now, giving Cassie space. But his gaze felt heavy. I shifted on my paws. We were digging up horrible memories. For everyone. "But you know how it is, procedures . . ."

Suddenly Cassie's shoulders dropped. Her eyes got all shiny. I hated when they did that. Only I could smell that the pooling tears weren't real, that they were part of an act. She wasn't actually starting to cry. She was digging deeper.

"Yeah, Mom just can't believe someone would try to set her up like that. Blame her. After all we, I mean she, has been through, losing Uncle Mark and all." She bent down and hugged me around the neck. Hiding. I could feel her peeking up through my fur to see how the act was working. I tried to make my fur fluff up, to help her. She was out on a limb. The Chief hadn't said anything about being set up.

The idea didn't seem new to Langtree, though. He nodded and frowned. He sighed heavily but kept his mouth shut. He was done talking.

"I'll just put these on her desk," Cassie said, sniffing. She stood up, walked to The Chief's door, and slid the big key into the lock. I heard a click. Bingo!

But Langtree got to his feet, to follow us. "Oh, I can take those." He held out his hand. Cassie took two quick steps and handed him the keys while I stayed and held the door open.

"Is it okay if I just get my mom's phone charger? She left it here by accident." Cassie asked but didn't wait for an answer. She dashed inside before Langtree could stop her. She set her bag on The Chief's chair and I used my snout to spin it around so the high back blocked Langtree's view. Nice work.

Moving quickly, Cassie pulled a charger and her phone out of her bag, keeping them both in one hand. She rifled through a few items on the desk, sniffing for clues. She snapped a few photos with her phone.

She was so busy clicking she didn't see Langtree getting up from his chair. I had her back, though. I ran interference, meeting him at the door.

He petted me but didn't bend down. Didn't look at my face. I could tell I wouldn't be able to hold him for long. Cassie could tell, too, now that she was done clicking. She held up the charger like she'd just grabbed it from the drawer.

"Here it is!" She waved the cord at Langtree and dropped it into her pack. *Woof!* Good work, Cassie.

She walked toward us, and we strolled out the door, all wags. Mission accomplished!

# CHAPTER 6

I pulled the door to Mom's office closed behind me, making sure it was locked. That was close! My heart was thudding so hard I was sure everyone around me could hear it. But thanks to Dodge I got a look at a few things — and even some photos of photos on Mom's desk.

I forced my face into an innocent smile and looked up at Officer Langtree. "Mom'll be really glad to have —"

The phone on Langtree's desk rang, and he dashed over to answer it, sparing me the explanation. I waved and started for the door. I felt tingly with excitement and was already outside in my head when Dodge suddenly tensed and sped up.

"Easy," I whispered. If we raced out of there we'd look guilty! But as soon as the word was out of my mouth, I saw why he was itching to make a run for it. Hero and his officer, Hank Riley, had just rounded the cubicle corner and were heading right toward us.

I quickened my pace, but it was too late. Hero had spotted *his* hero and was straining like a maniac to get to Dodge. Dodge looked up at me with a help-me expression, and I felt for him. But what could I do?

"Sorry, boy," I whispered. "We've got to act casual."

With a silent sigh Dodge sat down on his haunches and waited for the attack. I turned toward the duo, trying not to look irritated, and nearly laughed out loud. Talk about comic relief! Not only was Hero bouncing up to Dodge like he was spring-loaded, his nails sliding all over the tile floor, he had some crazy contraption strapped to his head. The young shepherd looked even goofier than usual.

*Lick, lick, lick.* Hero's tongue was all over Dodge's face, and he nearly poked him in the eye with the antenna that stuck out of the thing on his head. When Dodge didn't react (he suffered the slobber admirably), Hero went full belly-up on the office floor. I couldn't help but laugh. He wanted Dodge to like him so badly! Dodge, though, was not amused.

"Hey there, Cassie," Officer Riley said, sidling up to us with an odd grin. Dodge eyed him warily, and I agreed. There was something about this guy that didn't sit right — something I couldn't quite put my finger on. As he stood there grinning at me, I suddenly realized that if what I'd been implying to Langtree was true — that Mom had been set up — Riley could be a suspect. Everyone in this place could be a suspect! Riley, Deb, Langtree. Everyone! My mind started spinning, thinking about inside jobs.

"Oh, hey, Officer Riley," I replied, trying not to let my thoughts show.

Riley tugged on Hero's leash, and he rolled back onto his belly. "Did you see our new FIDO?"

"FIDO?" I asked.

"Yeah, it stands for Firearm Intervention and Dangerous Operations. It's a dog cam. Anything Hero sees I see on this screen here." He proudly tapped the small screen he was carrying, which at the moment showed a strange upside-down view of Dodge's chin. "I've been wanting to get my hands on one of these for a long time. It took forever, but we finally got a replacement for the one Dodge lost — er, well, it just came in the mail."

Dodge shifted on his paws, looking miserable. Hero sat up and I bent down to check out the device strapped between his ears. It was a little crooked but looked super high-tech, with a camera lens and infrared lights for seeing at night. I didn't want to seem overly interested and start some long conversation, though. So I pretended to be a little bored while Riley beamed at me like a kid with a new toy.

Then, quick as a wink, his expression changed to one of concern. "So, uh, how is your mom doing?" he asked, shifting on his feet. "I feel just terrible about what happened."

Dodge cocked his head to the side — he was suspicious. Both of us were wondering if Riley *should* be feeling terrible. I put my hand on Dodge's head and nodded at Riley while he yammered on about Mom's "unfortunate

45

situation." He was so awkward and nervous I couldn't tell if he was being sincere. Or not.

"Anyway, uh, I'm sure it'll all get straightened out soon." Riley finally trailed off.

Hero dropped low again, trying to get Dodge's attention, and the camera slipped farther. If Dodge noticed, he didn't show it. His eyes were glued on Riley.

"Yeah, I'm sure she'll be back here cracking the whip before we know it," he added. He didn't sound convincing.

*Play it cool,* I told Dodge silently. Dodge heard me and looked away, feigning boredom. He even yawned. Good dog.

"Speaking of *The Chief*," I said, emphasizing Mom's suspended title and trying to sound breezy, "I'd better get home before she puts an all-points bulletin out on me and Dodge. We just came by to drop off her keys." I smiled at my joke, and Riley threw back his head and laughed loudly. Too loudly.

I patted my leg, and Dodge was instantly by my side. "See you," I said to Riley over his guffaws. We headed toward the door and left the laughing policeman and his whimpering dog behind us.

It was good to get outside. Really good, actually. I took a deep breath, inhaling the late afternoon air, and Dodge did a full-body shake.

We turned onto Third Street, my mind whirring like a blender. "If Mom's been set up, it definitely could have been an inside job," I told Dodge as he trotted steadily beside me. "Which means that *everyone* in that station is a suspect." I saw his ears twitching. He was listening, like always, and I wondered if he was having as much trouble swallowing this situation as I was. "And Officer Riley seemed pretty darn suspicious. . . ."

"Woof!" Dodge let out a sharp bark, finishing my sentence and agreeing with me all at once.

"Glad we're thinking along the same lines," I said with a nod. "When we get home, we'll make some notes and see what we come up with, okay boy?"

I glanced down in time to see Dodge peel away from my side and sprint down the alley by the Smokehouse. "Dodge? Dodge, come on. We've got to get home."

My partner ignored me completely — totally unlike him. "Dodge!" I called, rushing forward and squinting in the dusk. I could make out his moving tail, his nose pressed into the gap behind a Dumpster. I heard a growl. Was that Dodge, or another animal? I couldn't see anything. "What is it?" I asked, coming up behind him. His body was tense. "What do you see?" I asked again. A low growl was the only answer I got.

# CHAPTER 7

I wasn't on my game. At all. Maybe seeing Hero in the camera threw me — brought back too many memories. Maybe I was losing my edge. Didn't matter, really. The point was, the perp got away. Again.

"Woof!" I barked at the gap behind the Dumpster. "Woof! Woof! Rarwf!" The gap was too small for me to fit through.

Cassie tried to calm me down. Her hand caressed the fur on my neck, and her voice was quiet. "What is it? Did you see someone?"

Not some*one*. Some*dog*. And I didn't see him, I smelled him. The Burger Burglar. I got a good whiff. I was certain.

He was in there, and he was hiding. I stood. Staring. Wagging. Waiting. But he wasn't coming out.

"Let's go, Dodge," Cassie said. "We've got to get home." But I didn't want to go. I was a little wound up. Wound up and getting nowhere. So I let her lead me away from the gap. Away from the Burger Burglar.

She couldn't lead me away from my thoughts, though. My thoughts about Hero with the FIDO. And Officer Riley. Cassie was right about him — he was too anxious. Laughed too loud. Tried too hard. Wanted to be liked too much.

Sometimes, when dogs really wanted to be liked, they did bad things. Really bad things. Like taking out the dogs above them. My old partner used to be above Riley, and now Riley had his job. My hackles rose. I didn't like to think about that.

Maybe if I'd been able to stop thinking about that, I might have been able to warn Cassie about what was going to happen next. We might have been able to avoid it completely. But I was distracted. I didn't see it coming. See *her* coming. Didn't smell her, either. Cassie's Least Favorite Person, Summer Hill. Summer Hill set Cassie's hackles on end. If my girl was a dog, she'd show her teeth to Summer on sight. And I could see why. Summer held her nose in the air. She said mean things. She even got me banned from Cassie's school. *Grrrr.*

Cassie sucked in a breath when Summer came into view. She resisted the urge to turn and run. Good girl. Cassie hated Summer Hill, but running away would make her look like a coward. It would also look ridiculous. Cassie was brave, smart, and scrappy. Summer was a prissy girl who dressed in ridiculous outfits that matched her dog's.

Summer's dog, Muffet, trotted next to her on the end of a rhinestone leash. She wore booties and a doggie vest with puff-ball fringe. And if that weren't enough to make a dog tuck tail and crawl under the porch, Summer was sporting fluffy pom-pom boots and a matching, girl-size vest. They were dressed like a pair of identical cat toys. I wasn't sure who looked sillier. But I *was* sure that Muffet didn't dress herself. . . .

I stuck close to Cassie as we approached the ridiculous duo. I could hear my girl's teeth grinding. She was probably clamping them together to keep from saying something she'd regret. Too bad Summer could never do the same.

"Hi Cassssssandra," Summer hissed when we got close. I hated the way she said my girl's name. Cassie did, too, but she didn't respond.

"I heard about your mom losing her job," Summer whined. She stuck her lip out and made a sad face. I could smell the laugh behind it. "I'm sooo sorry," she added, blinking rapidly.

I clamped my mouth shut. The girl made me want to growl. She didn't sound sorry. Not at all. I was thinking about plucking a pom-pom off of her boots with my teeth when I was interrupted by a yip from Muffet. I'd been purposely ignoring the kid. Trying to spare her the embarrassment of being seen by another dog in her current, uh, state. But the Maltese was asking for attention. She barked and strained on her sparkling leash. She was shaking with excitement. She probably didn't get to see many real dogs up close.

Summer yanked her back, but Muffet kept yapping. She rose up on her hind legs to give me a good nose-to-tail sniff. I stepped closer and let her catch a good whiff. Why not? A dog had to do what a dog had to do. Even a prissy bit of a dog like Miss Muffet.

"Muffet! No!" Summer jerked the little dog back, horrified. Muffet ignored her. Her tiny tail wagged like it was in a wind storm.

"Gross. Get away from . . . ewww!" Summer stopped pulling on the leash and bent over to pick up Muffet. For a microdog, the Maltese had some staying power. "Come on, Muffie. Let's get away from these . . . mutts!"

Pom-poms bouncing, Summer marched up the street with Muffet struggling in her arms. Cassie let out a giggle — the most noise she'd made since we left the Smokehouse. I gave a bark. We didn't mind being called mutts. Not a bit. Mutts were gutsy and full of surprises. Mutts survived. But our laugh didn't last. It faded quickly, and Cassie's jaw stayed shut the rest of the way home. She walked fast and said nothing. She was thinking. We both were. Thinking about Summer and Muffet. Hero and Riley. The Mom and getting home. Yes, getting home. I was looking forward to getting home.

Only I was so busy thinking about getting home that I forgot what being home was like. When we walked in, I was assaulted by the bad smells that were quickly becoming normal. Sharp, pungent odors that made my hackles go up. Not just cleaning products. No. I smelled a fight.

"Easy, Dodge." Cassie ran her hand over my upright fur, trying to smooth it. Trying to calm me down. She took a few steps, scanning the kitchen, looking in the living room.

I huffed, getting used to the smell, and tried to put my fur flat. I didn't want Cassie to think she was in danger. Not that kind of danger, anyway. I just wanted her to know something was up.

A light shone under the office door, on the far side of the living room. The Mom and The Dad were in there with the door closed. Cassie walked closer, and I followed silently.

The Sullivans didn't usually shut each other out, but when a door was closed, it meant that someone wanted privacy. Dogs don't do privacy. And even if we did, a door wouldn't cut it. It took more than a slab of wood to hide smells and voices from a canine. Even when people were whispering their shouts.

"The accusations are baseless, Joe!" The Mom said. She was irritated, hissing her *s*'s. "I was as surprised as you are. But there's nothing we can do now except wait and watch our budget."

I understood the no-eavesdropping rule. I really did. And so did Cassie. But the whisper-shouts coming through the office door were impossible to ignore. I couldn't help what I heard. And Cassie couldn't help it if she felt like sitting down for minute. Right there. Behind the couch. Really close to the door.

I lay down next to Cassie and made myself as small as possible — not very small — and stayed still.

I could hear Cassie's heart pumping fast, and I licked her hand.

"For how long?" The Dad asked. He sounded done. Tired.

There was a pause. I heard feet on carpet. Then The Mom spoke again. "Sometimes these investigations take months."

"Months?" The Dad squeaked like the fake plastic burger toys at Pet Rescue. "We can't live on my salary alone."

"Mayor Baudry said he'd try to get my pay reinstated." The Mom was trying to sound upbeat, but I could smell the truth. She wasn't upbeat. She was beaten down.

"Yeah, and Baudry *always* makes good on his promises," The Dad retorted. He wasn't bothering to whisper. And he used that tone that meant the opposite of what he was saying.

"It's going to be okay," The Mom insisted. Now she sounded annoyed.

Cassie was barely breathing. I leaned into her. Propped her up as best I could.

"No, Dorrie. It's not. It's never going to be okay. Mark is *dead*." There was a long silence. Thick and deep.

"This isn't my fault," The Mom said. Her voice was high and clipped, like the short, sharp bark of a Chihuahua. "How can I expect the force to believe me if my own husband won't?"

Dead silence. It stretched on for a long time.

"Maybe you can't." The words were hanging there when the door flew open and The Dad stormed out of the office. He rushed past us, nearly stepping on my tail, and stormed out the front door. If he'd seen us, he showed no sign. I felt my legs twitch, wanting to run after him. But I stayed. I was a good dog.

Cassie's body was clenched tight next to me. I stifled a whimper in my throat.

"This seriously sucks," a voice said in the darkness. I whipped my head around to see where the voice had come from. A foot stuck out from behind the big reading chair by the window. It was wearing Sam's sequined sneaker.

"What are you doing back there?" Cassie hissed.

"Eavesdropping, same as you," Sam shot back. "You're not the only one around here with sleuthing skills."

Cassie exhaled v-e-r-y slowly. She made a decision. "So, what'd I miss?"

Sam scooched closer. Her face looked pinched. "Not much. Mom told Dad that we'll have to cut corners. I think Dad grumbled something about blind corners, but it was hard to hear. He sounded really mad."

Suddenly the door to the office reopened, wide this time. We were caught in a shaft of light. The Mom blinked and looked down at us. Her face was blotchy. "Oh, girls," she said quietly. "I didn't know you were there. . . ." Her voice trailed off and she just stood there, shoulders slumped.

Sam jumped to her feet and threw her arms around The Mom, sobbing. The Mom patted her shoulder. "It's going to be all right, Samantha," she said as she led her toward the kitchen. But she wasn't convincing anyone.

Cassie watched them go with shiny eyes, and this time it wasn't an act. Then she got to her feet, shook herself a little, and walked into the office. I wasn't sure what she was up to, so I waited by the sofa. The Sister came out of the kitchen and walked upstairs. My stomach rumbled.

When Cassie finally came out of the office, there was a funny lump under her sweatshirt. A bone? I wagged. I sniffed. No, not a bone. Paper.

"Come on," she whispered as she started up the stairs. I followed, even though it was almost time for dinner. *Dinner, dinner, dinner.* And I was hungry.

I wasn't through the door when I smelled company. The Cat. In our room. *Grrr.* Then I saw The Sister huddled up on Cassie's bed. With The Cat. The Cat was stretched out like she owned the joint. The Sister's face was still a mess. Her eyes were shiny, too. Cassie climbed onto the bed and gave her sister a hug. The Sister sniffled and leaned into my girl. They didn't always get along, but they were littermates. And they were cuddling for comfort.

I eyed The Cat — no comfort there — and lay down on my bed to wait for dinner.

# CHAPTER 8

"It's going to be okay," I said, squeezing Sam's shoulders. Maybe Mom was onto something.

Sam sat up a little and sniffled loudly. "You think so?"

"Yes," I said. But I was biting my lip, because I wasn't sure. I wasn't sure at all. The situation was bad, and didn't look like it would be getting better anytime soon. But my little sister didn't need to know that — at least not right now.

"It's just that Mom is acting so weird, and Dad is so angry all the time. . . ."

"I know, but it'll be over soon." I paused. It was probably best to change the subject altogether, to distract her. "Did you get a chance to start on your science project?"

Sam's eyes widened. "Oh my God, the science project!" she groaned. "I totally forgot!" She jumped up,
sending Furball to the floor and startling Dodge. I handed
her a tissue. "You think I can get started before dinner?"
she asked.

"Sure," I said. "I don't think dinner will be ready for a
while." I felt sort of bad for rushing her out of my room. It
wasn't that long ago that it was her room, too, and she was
having a hard time. But I couldn't stop thinking about the
folder I'd just borrowed from the office. I'd shoved it
under a pile of stuff on my desk when I came in, so Sam
wouldn't see it. But one thing was clear: The fastest way
out of the funk my family had fallen into was to get to the
bottom of Mom's suspension. To be honest, I was pretty
shaken by Mom and Dad's fighting, too. I knew Dad
missed Uncle Mark like crazy and that he'd never been
happy about how dangerous Mom's job was. But even if
Dad was doubting Mom, I wasn't. I could fix this, and I
would, just as soon as I got Sam out of my room.

Sam took the tissue and blew her nose like a trumpet,
then smiled weakly. "Thanks, Cass."

I gave her a hug. "Anytime." She leaned down and

scooped up Furball, then headed out. I crossed the carpet on her heels, closing the door tightly behind her and leaning against it. I was exhausted, but the file had to go back ASAP, so there was no time to rest.

"We've got to get to work," I told Dodge. He thumped his tail on the rug while I got my case notebook out of my backpack. I sat down on the floor and leaned against the bed, thinking. I desperately wanted to dig into that file but knew I should make notes first, while my visit to the station was fresh in my mind. Pushing all thoughts of Summer, Dad, and Sam out of my mind, I turned to an empty page and wrote: "Mom's Suspension" at the top, then made a list of station suspects below that.

CHASE LANGTREE: Mom's assistant for two years. Seems a little cagey. Is he happy working for Mom? Anxious for promotion? Has full access to Mom's work files, i.e., opportunity to set her up!

DEB BRUBAKER: Seems friendly. Motive? Mom made her pay several parking tickets she wanted to wiggle out of — did that make her angry? Access to files unclear.

DOUG WALKER: Where was he today? Often works with Mom on cases. Access to inside information. They seem to have a good relationship. . . .

HANK RILEY: Totally suspicious. Laughs too loud. Been at the station a long time, knows the ins and outs; would probably know how to get his hands on files/info that he wouldn't have official access to. Took Uncle Mark's job and office.

I looked over at Dodge, because I knew how hard it was for him to lose his partner. And his job. I knew what he'd been through. Leaning down, I gave him a kiss on the forehead. "It's behind you now," I said soothingly, even though a lot of it was being dug back up. There were more officers to include on my list, but I was anxious to get to the next part of our investigation.

Dodge leaned against my leg and I closed the notebook, reaching for the thick folder. There were pages and pages inside, clipped together in sections. The top one was labeled "Confidential: Corps Investigation."

"I think this calls for extra security," I said, getting up to lock my door. Settling back down next to Dodge, I started to spread the Corps Investigation papers on the carpet. There were the articles I'd seen and some memos and pictures of men, apparently Corps members. I'd never heard of most of them, but one rang a bell: Gerard Slatterly — an older, greasy-looking guy. He had a thick neck, a round, puffy face, and sparse, slicked-back hair. He was the guy pointed out in the Post-it at the opening of the community center. But I also had the feeling I'd seen him somewhere else.

I leafed through a few more photos. Notes beneath the faces told me that all of these men were suspected of racketeering, which I had to look up online to understand. It sounded like something you did with tennis gear, but actually meant using a business to cover up crimes or hide money that was earned illegally. Mafia stuff. From the police memos, I could tell that Mom and Uncle Mark had been investigating each of these criminals independently, trying to link them to The Corps, but hadn't had much luck. They were gathering info and planning a raid on The Corps's suspected headquarters. That raid was supposed to provide the evidence they needed to put these guys away. That was the raid that went wrong. Everything the police hoped to find was destroyed in the awful, unexplained explosion. The crooks went free, and Uncle Mark . . .

I didn't realize I was crying until Dodge licked my face with his big pink tongue. I gulped and leaned into him, absorbing his warmth. Then I wiped my cheeks and got up. It was way past our regular dinnertime, but Mom hadn't called me to set the table. Was there even going to *be* dinner? The house was unusually quiet. I unlocked my door and snuck downstairs to put the folder back where I found it. My mind was on overdrive, thinking about the raid. What caused the explosion? Why was Uncle Mark alone? And what was The Corps up to now?

Dodge cocked his head, pricking his ears. Dad was home. I shoved the folder to the bottom of the pile on the desk and listened to the front door close. I waited to hear voices, but it was totally silent. I hoped Sam was making good progress on her report, at least. I hoped Owen was doing okay downstairs in his room. Maybe he was stuffing his ears with extra loud music to drown everything out. I reached for Dodge and he put his chin on my thigh, letting out a long exhale. I totally agreed. I wished I could tune everything out, too — everything except my dog.

# CHAPTER 9

"Whoa. Twelve burgers?" Hayley eyed the giant bag of hamburgers I was holding, her expression a combination of disbelief and shock. "I know you like to eat, but twelve?"

Smiling to myself, I shrugged in response. It wasn't very often that I got to pull something over on my best human friend. "I do it all the time." I said. Ha! Whenever I rescued strays, I meant.

Hayley's eyes got so huge and bulgy I had to come clean before they popped out of her head. "They're not for me," I admitted. "They're for the dogs down on the waterfront."

Hayley just kept looking at me, so I explained. "There are loads of strays down there, and I've been helping Taylor catch them and bring them to Pet Rescue. If we don't bring them in, the city will nab them, and that would mean —"

Hayley covered her ears, her head moving from side to side. "Don't say it! I *know* what it would mean." She shuddered.

"Exactly," I agreed. "Too terrible to think about. That's why I've been doing a little Pet Rescue overtime. That, and because I need to get out of my house as much as possible." I was trying to joke but couldn't even smile. Hayley gave me a sympathetic look and I caved. "It's like last year all over again, only worse," I confessed. "And . . ." I hesitated. I knew she remembered how it was at 332 Salisbury Drive after Uncle Mark died, when we were a family of mourning zombies. It was so awful, I honestly hadn't known if we were going to make it through. Then Dodge moved in and basically saved my life. Hayley had been there for me then, too, so I figured I owed her the whole truth. "And now Mom's been accused of being the one who caused Uncle Mark's death," I said in a rush. It felt good to finally tell her, and also horrible to say it out loud.

Hayley just stared at me while my words sank in. Then she put her arm around my shoulders. "We both know that can't be true," she said. "Not in a million years."

I exhaled. Good answer. It was exactly what I wanted — and needed — to hear. But even though it made me feel better, it also made me feel worse. Because right now my little sister, who looked like the walking dead at breakfast, was at home . . . alone. I wondered if she was doing okay. I looked down at Dodge, who was drooling at the sight of the burger bag, and gave him a pat. "Sorry, boy. I think I'm going to have to take you home. Sam needs the company, and you do make those strays anxious." I dropped to my knees and gave him a hug. "But only because they don't know what a cupcake you are," I added.

I straightened and turned to Hayley. "*You* could come with me, though," I said hopefully. In addition to being the best baker in town, Hayley also loved dogs. Tragically, her parents wouldn't let her get one because, well, they just weren't dog people.

"I'd love to," she said.

"Great. We can use all the help we can get. I just have to drop Dodge at my house first and . . ." I looked down and realized my dog was no longer next to me. I checked around the corner by the Dumpster where he'd gone a little nutso the night before . . . and spotted the tip of his brown tail.

"Dodge!" I called. "Come on!"

Dodge took a final sniff and heeled, and Hayley and I got on our bikes. Ten minutes later the three of us were at my house.

"Hey, Sam," I called from the door.

Sam was working on her science project with her iPod on, and barely looked up. Even though I was a little annoyed, I couldn't really blame her — tuning out was a survival method we were all using.

"Go lie down," I whispered to Dodge. He gave me a pathetic look when he realized he wasn't coming out with me and Hayley, so I reached into the bag for a meaty treat.

"Just one," I warned, knowing he could have eaten the whole dozen in two minutes flat. He sniffed the bun and ate it first.

"I know, I know — poor consolation prize," I agreed. I crouched next to him and met his eyes. "But I need you to stay here for Sam. You're taking one for Team Sullivan." Mom wasn't home at the moment, but she was still commanding Operation Clean. And Dad had been putting in as much overtime as he could to earn a little extra income. *And to stay away from Mom*, I thought with a worried pang.

Licking his chops, Dodge headed into the living room. He spun three times, then lay down near Sam's feet, as far from Furball as possible. Sam didn't look up at me but did reach down to give Dodge a welcoming pet, so I know it helped.

Outside, Hayley and I hopped on our bikes and rode to the waterfront. I was so happy to escape the house — even without Dodge — that everything looked fresh and crisp. When we got to Rhoda Street, I started to see signs on a bunch of warehouses — signs I'd never noticed before. PROPERTY OF GREENWAY INDUSTRIES, they said over a picture of little high-rise buildings sprouting leaves. It looked familiar.

I remembered seeing GreenWay's name and logo at the community center — they must have been big donors or something. The logos had been all over Bellport last year, on signs urging people to vote for Measure G. Measure G was supposed to use tax money to build a new park in the warehouse district, the start of a greenbelt.

"Hey, look. 'Future Home of Seaway Greenbelt,'" Hayley read one of the warehouse signs out loud like she was reading my mind. "It'll be great when we finally get that park. The views out here are gorgeous, but there's no place to hang out and enjoy them. It's almost like a ghost town."

I nodded. Something about the signs gave me an uneasy feeling, and I pedaled a little harder. Every warehouse with a sign on it seemed to be abandoned. Empty and run-down. Not the park-like pedestrian setting GreenWay used in their Measure G ads.

A few minutes later we found Taylor in the same spot he'd been three days before, sitting on the edge of the loading dock with spiderwebs in his hair.

"Hey," he called to us. "I hope you brought your magic, because it's tough going today."

I smiled and wagged the bag in the air. "Sure did," I replied. "And Taylor, this is Hayley. Hayley, Taylor." I heard myself saying their names out loud and was shocked to realize they'd never met. How was that possible?

"Good to meet you," Taylor said in his usual friendly way.

Hayley nodded, but her face looked a little weird and she was uncharacteristically silent. I was wondering what that meant when Taylor let out a sigh and stretched his legs.

"I need a break," he admitted. "I've been working on the same dogs we were trying to lure the other day, and they're not budging. I feel like I've been under there for hours. Do you think you guys could give it a try?"

Hayley nodded emphatically but still didn't say anything, and a few minutes later we were belly down, crawling as far under the low deck as we could get. As my eyes adjusted, I saw four shiny spots from two pairs of eyes and heard a shuffling whimper.

"You know you're hungry," I said softly. "It's okay. We won't hurt you."

The dogs scooched closer. They were so cute. And so skinny! I saw their noses quivering, smelling the food. They wanted burgers. They needed burgers. They inched forward slowly. I . . . thought . . . they . . . were . . . almost . . . to . . . me . . . and . . .

They were gone! The puppies retreated back under the building so far I couldn't see them at all. What the heck?

A wave of frustration crashed over me and I looked back toward Taylor and the light. That's when I saw them: the boots. As in Taylor's big, black boots. To a puppy (who'd probably felt the front side of a shoe before), they'd be huge. Monstrous, even.

"I think it's your boots," I called to Taylor as Hayley and I began to crawl out. "What if they're afraid of them?" I squinted in the light and brushed a strand of cobwebby hair out of my eyes.

"Oh, man," Taylor groaned, glancing down at his signature footwear. "I didn't even think of that!" Sitting down on the blacktop, he pulled his boots off and set them out of view. He was wearing mismatched socks — one white and one funky print — and Hayley giggled. Not just a little "that's silly" snarfle, either. She let out one of those twittery giggles like she was Snow White and had birds alighting on her shoulders. What was *that*?

Hayley was no giggler. Milk-out-her-nose laugher? Yes. Giggler? No. I glanced back at Taylor, who was pretty much the best guy friend I had, and it suddenly dawned on me that he was not only really nice and really committed to animals, he was also *cute*. And that Hayley obviously thought he was super, *duper*, cute. *Oh, man!*

I was trying to wrap my head around these two lightning bolt thoughts when Officer Riley and Hero appeared around the corner of the warehouse. *Really?* I thought. *Now?* Riley was in street clothes; the pair was clearly off duty. Only Hero was wearing the stupid FIDO camera and bounded up to me, sniffing wildly.

Riley squared his shoulders and adopted his policeman expression. "What are you kids doing down here?" he asked. "This is not a good place to play."

Play? Please! Did he think we had a bag of Barbies with us? I considered bluffing, but Taylor took charge. "We're working, actually — trying to rescue stray dogs that have been abandoned," he said, pulling out his Pet Rescue ID. I was totally grateful that he'd thought to bring it, even though the sight of it made Haley's admiring eyes grow even wider.

I wanted to ask Riley what *he* was doing down here. After all, it wasn't "a good place to play," and he hardly seemed to be working. But I didn't want to seem too interested in his comings and goings. So I asked about the camera instead. "I see Hero is wearing the FIDO. Are you getting any good footage?"

Riley cleared his throat. "Um, yes. We're just, um, practicing with it out in the field," he mumbled. I was instantly suspicious. As a rule, police property wasn't supposed to be used off duty.

"Yeah, I suppose there are a lot of empty buildings around here to explore. . . ." I stopped talking, because I suddenly spotted a pair of dark noses poking out from under the loading dock. The pups! Now that the boots were off, they'd come almost all the way out of hiding! I reached for a burger for extra enticement, but at that moment Hero smelled the other dogs and went berserk.

"Rwoof! Rwoof! Rwoof!"

He strained hard on the leash, and Riley pulled him back. "Hero, no!"

But it was too late. The pair of pups disappeared and we were back to square one. Ugh!

# CHAPTER 10

Hanging out with The Sister wasn't too bad except for one thing: She smelled like The Cat. Which made my nose itch and bugged like a flea under my collar. Not that she could help it — that thing slept on her bed. They were bound to share a scent.

On the other hand, The Sister loved brushing fur — my fur. And that almost made up for The Cat smell. A good brushing was like a good pet and a good scratch all rolled together. *Woof.* I loved a good brushing.

The Sister brushed me for so long that I forgot to think about Cassie. Forgot to wonder what she was doing. I let go. Let my muscles go soft. Let my mind off-leash. When she finally stopped brushing and switched on the TV, I lay there. Relaxed. Then The Cat jumped onto The Sister's lap, flicking my snout with her tail. My nose twitched, making me *un*relax. I got up and took a stroll to the kitchen for some crumb patrol. Nobody likes a dirty floor.

The Brother was already in the food zone. His stomach was growling (I can hear these things) and his whole head was in the fridge. He was lucky. He could open the giant treat box without help.

"Hey, D," The Brother greeted. I gave a wag, and wagged harder when he straightened. He was totally loaded down with food. So loaded he had to close the fridge with his foot. He set the grub on the counter. I couldn't see everything that was up there, but I smelled the good stuff: bread, mayo, cheese, and . . . I breathed in deep so the smell would hit the back of my throat, so it would feel almost like eating a mouthful of . . . salami! I loved salami. Salami was my favorite.

The Brother looked my way and I licked my chops. To

remind him how much I enjoyed sandwiches. Especially the insides.

"How's it going?" he asked. The Brother was never perky. He moved slowly. Spoke softly. Grumbled a lot. He was a laid-back guy. "This stuff making you crazy, too?"

Was he talking about the pile of yum on the counter? Or the way the Sullivan Pack was acting? I wasn't sure, but it didn't matter. The answer was yes. *Yes! Yes! Yes!* He pulled a knife loaded with mayo out of the jar. My eyes locked on the creamy, delicious blob. I might have whined. I definitely drooled.

"Right?" he said, looking at me. "Me, too. It sucks when things are messed up. It sucks when your mom makes you scrub the floor with a toothbrush. It sucks when your parents aren't talking to each other. It all *sucks.*" Oh, that stuff. I knew what he was talking about now but couldn't take my eyes off the knife. The mayo was about to plop onto the floor.

The Brother topped his sandwich with a second slice of bread and carried it to the table. He slumped into a chair. He took a bite and chewed. I rubbed against his leg and rested my chin on his thigh.

"Thanks, D." He patted my head and took another bite. I watched the sandwich move from the plate to his mouth. Plate. Mouth. Plate. Mouth. A piece of salami was sticking out on one side. I wiggled and licked my chops.

Finally he set the last of his sandwich on the floor. Finally! It was gone in a single bite.

"Glad you enjoyed that," The Brother said with a chuckle. He ruffed up my neck fur. "You're a good listener, Dodge. Best one in the house." He put the plate in the dishwasher and went down the stairs to his den. I considered following him. I liked his den. But now that I was up and had gobbled down a little snack, I was thinking about Cassie. Hard at work without me. I barked at the back door, and The Sister came to open it for me. I waited until she was out of sight, then jumped the fence. Even though Cassie told me not to come, I had to go.

I ran through the neighborhood, not bothering with my usual sniffing and news gathering. When I got to Pet Rescue, I slipped into stealth mode. Stealth mode was all about moving slow. Not being seen. Taking everything in. Sights. Sounds. Smells. Stealthy.

I passed warehouses, most of them empty. I passed abandoned cars, all empty. I smelled some garbage. Old garbage. Stinky delicious. And other stuff: mildew, dust, grease, rats. I even caught sight of a disappearing rodent tail.

Skirting the side of an abandoned building, I heard a car engine. Then voices. I slunk up along the metal wall, peeked around the corner, and pulled back. My nose and eyes got the information at the same time: Hero and Riley were here. With someone who smelled like a meatball sub.

I peeked again and noted some stuff. The meatball sub held an armful of signs with leafy buildings on them. Riley wasn't in uniform. But Hero wore the FIDO. His nose twitched.

Any second now my replacement would smell me and go nuts. It was time to head out. I doubled back the way I came, then turned down an alley. I listened for Cassie's voice. I sniffed for burgers. But I didn't smell anything good, and what I heard was the sound of . . . paws?

Yes. Four paws trotted along the pavement behind me in a rhythm just a little faster than mine. I sped up. So did the steps. I slowed down. The steps slowed, too. Was Hero following me? Maybe I hadn't gotten away fast enough. Or maybe it was the Burger Burglar!

I turned down another alley and heard my tracker turn, too. I needed to get a look, or at least a smell, of whoever it was. I needed the wind at my back. I turned again and the breeze brought me the information. It wasn't Hero. Or the Burger Burglar. My four-footed pursuer smelled like flowers and nail polish and . . .

Summer Hill! I whirled around and saw Muffet, Summer's tiny Maltese, half a block back. She stopped when I turned, but stood her ground. Trying not to tremble in the shadow of the building. Her girl was not with her. She wore a sparkly collar with a chewed-off bit of leash still attached. The puny pup had busted out. Gotten free. Run away. Who could blame her? She was probably sick of wearing sweaters. Just the thought of playing dress-up made me drop fur. How humiliating.

I was having other feelings looking at her, too. Lots of them. Annoyance: I'd lost time getting to Cassie. Admiration: For a petite pooch, Muffet had pluck. Worry: The docks were no place for a pampered pet.

"Grrr." I growled at Muffet, telling her to go home. *Go!* She lifted a paw to step back, but didn't. I growled again. It wasn't safe for her here. Still, she stayed. Pluck.

*Aw, woof.* If I couldn't scare her, I'd have to lose her. I whirled and took off at a run. Not my fastest. How hard could it be to lose a Maltese? Muffet was smaller than The Cat. I did a zigzag down a side street, around a row of Dumpsters, and past a pair of cargo containers. I thought that would do it, but I could hear without turning that Muffet was still on my tail. I jumped onto a pile of pallets. I leaped onto a loading dock. I cleared the Dumpster beside it. I heard Muffet scramble onto the pile behind me. There was no way she'd make the jump. No way she'd even try. I stopped to look back. I was right and I was wrong. She jumped. And missed. I heard her land in the Dumpster with a squishy plop. *Woof.*

My ears drooped. The tiny dog's moxie had gotten her in deep, but I hadn't exactly helped. Which meant I had to help now.

I walked back to the edge of the loading dock and looked into the Dumpster. It was ripe with smells. Rotted broccoli. Rancid potatoes. Liquid lettuce. And there, in the middle of it, was Muffet. She yipped at me and clawed at the slimy metal walls, but I was helpless. I couldn't reach her, couldn't help her out. I had to call for backup. I threw my head back and barked out the alarm.

# CHAPTER 11

L iving on the street was tough on dogs. Hunger gnawed at them. Fear gnawed at them. Loneliness gnawed at them. The hunger was probably the worst. Hunger could drive a dog to do strange things, like accept a Smokehouse burger from the hand of a stranger.

Hero and Officer Riley hadn't been gone long when the smaller of the black-and-white pups, the female, crept into the light to grab the still-warm burger from my outstretched fingers. She took it gently, cautiously, then dragged it about a foot away and inhaled it as fast as she could. "Slow down," I said in a calm voice. "It's okay. I'm not going to take it back."

I held out another burger to her brother, whose quivering nose poked out of the shadows. Once he saw that his sister hadn't been hit or kicked or yelled at, he grew braver. He stretched his neck out, took the burger, and scarfed down his free meal with his tail tucked between his legs.

I offered the puppies two more burgers and inched closer while they ate them. "Everything's going to be fine," I soothed. The dogs were older than I thought — maybe close to a year. They were skinny and shaking. I could count every one of their ribs.

I looked up at Taylor and Hayley. Taylor was getting out leashes and a crate. Hayley was watching his every move. I turned back to the pups, who were chewing and keeping a wary eye on me. "It's okay," I said again. "We're here to —"

"Woof! Woof! Woof!" Three short, sharp barks echoed through the deserted neighborhood, making me sit up straight. They weren't just any barks; they were Dodge's barks. *Dodge's barks?* That didn't make sense. Dodge was supposed to be . . .

"I gotta go!" I stood up too fast, making the pups startle and run. Dang! We'd almost had them! But I couldn't worry about that right now — I had to get to Dodge. He wasn't supposed to be here, and I knew that bark. That bark meant trouble.

I heard it again, this time a little louder, and I shoved the bag of burgers at Hayley. "Here," I said. In a way I felt grateful to be out of there — away from Hayley's lovesick face. I ran past four warehouses and turned a corner to find Dodge hanging halfway in and halfway out of a Dumpster in front of Happy Produce — the place where we'd seen the two men arguing a few days before.

"What are you doing?" I panted. I could hear whimpering coming from inside the big metal bin. I thought Dodge had gotten stuck on the edge of the Dumpster, so I helped him down. But the whimpering didn't stop when he was back on all fours. Dodge cocked his head toward the Dumpster and I looked inside the can of gross. There was *another* dog in there, half buried in rotting vegetables.

At first I didn't recognize the little dog. Then I wished I hadn't. "Oh, no. Muffet?!" What was *she* doing here? Panicked, I looked around for her person, Summer — the last human I wanted to see — and quickly realized I would never spot her here. Not because she was hiding, but because Summer wouldn't be caught dead down by the docks. There was no place to shop and nobody to see in this neighborhood. Just trash and strays . . . and Muffet.

"Good boy," I told Dodge. I never would have heard the Maltese's pleas without his big bark. "But . . . Muffet?" I locked eyes with my dog, wondering how he'd gotten us into this little situation. He looked away.

Muffet let out a yip. "Don't worry," I called down to her. "We'll get you out of there." *Somehow.* I didn't exactly want to climb into the Dumpster and wasn't even sure I'd be able to get back out if I did. I was staring at Muffet, wondering what to do and trying not to gag, when Dodge emerged from the Happy Produce rolltop door carrying a long pole with a claw on the end, an industrial grabber thingy.

"Nice," I said, nodding. I peered back at Muffet, who appeared to be sinking in the muck. "And just in time. I think she's stuck in quick trash." I held out my hand, but before I could take the rescue pole, I heard something way worse than Muffet's whimper.

"Hey, you, get back here!" A man in an apron was coming after Dodge.

"Hang on, Muffet," I called before rushing over to intercept the guy.

"Come back with that, you thief!" the man shouted.

"Sorry, sir!" I yelled back to get the man's attention. "My dog's not trying to steal anything!" When he saw me, the man stopped chasing Dodge but still looked furious. He also looked familiar.

"That your dog?" he asked angrily.

I nodded. "Yes. I'm sorry, but we have a kind of . . . situation." Right on cue, Muffet barked from inside the Dumpster. "*That* dog is mine," I pointed at Dodge. "But the dog trapped in your Dumpster isn't."

The man squinted at me, and that's when I spotted Hayley coming around the corner of the warehouse. She took one look at Dodge with the grabber thingy and headed over to help.

"One of those strays is stuck in my trash?" the man asked. He took a handkerchief out of his pocket and swabbed his face. "Maybe you should just leave it in there."

That was the wrong answer for several reasons, but there wasn't time to get into it. "Well, this one's not a stray, exactly. She's actually a registered AKC pedigree. She belongs to a . . ." I stopped, because I couldn't bring myself to call Summer a "friend," even in an emergency. ". . . *person* I know."

I led the Not-So-Jolly-Green-Grocer over to view the prized Maltese, hoping Muffet still had her head above the sludge. He galumphed after me and peered into the Dumpster. Muffet's head was still visible, and Hayley was using the grabber pole to try and fish her out. Hayley moved the pole in close. She closed the claw on Muffet's collar and swung her onto the asphalt, setting her down gently.

"Catch of the day," Hayley laughed as Dodge let out a bark.

Muffet let out a pathetic yip and shook. Rotten produce goo flew everywhere.

The green grocer's scowl deepened as a blob hit his shoe. I took the pole from Hayley and wiped it off as best I could on my shirt. "Thank you, Mr., um . . ." I offered the man my hand. He shook it and introduced himself reluctantly.

"Albrici," he said. "Ernest Albrici."

"I'm Cassie," I said, leaving off my last name. "And this is Dodge and Hayley and Muffet." The trio stood in a line, smiling and looking innocent.

Mr. Albrici managed half a smile and accepted his pole. "This place is really going to the dogs," he mumbled, turning away. "Been here thirty years. Thirty years running my own business. But lately . . ."

I followed, trying to look innocent and curious. "What do you mean, sir?"

"It's going to the dogs," he repeated. "The neighborhood is falling apart. Most of my neighbors have been bought out. They tried to buy me out, too. But I'm not budging." He rapped the pole on the ground, punctuating his words.

As he pounded the asphalt, I realized why he looked familiar. He was the guy Dodge and I'd seen on Wednesday, having an argument with the other guy in the suit. And that guy in the suit . . .

My thoughts were interrupted by Muffet shaking again, as if she were fresh from a bath — only what she sent flying was *not* soapy suds.

"Gross!" Hayley squealed, wiping slime off her cheek.

Mr. Albrici scowled at the glops spotting his apron.

"I'm so sorry," I apologized. But he didn't answer. He just walked away, ducking under the Happy Produce door, mumbling about stray dogs and real estate vultures.

"Thank you, Mr. Albrici!" I called after him. Then I pulled out my phone and scrolled through my camera roll to one of the pictures I'd taken in Mom's office last week. I squinted at the fuzzy image of two men from the photo on her desk. The notes under the photo identified the man on the left as Gerard Slatterly. My misty memory identified him as the guy in the suit who'd been fighting with Mr. Albrici — that's why he looked familiar! My mind whirled. My thoughts needed sorting. I was thinking two things: suit guy was part of The Corps, and suit guy was no friend of Happy Produce. But before I could figure out if those things were connected, I heard somebody start to chuckle.

"Summer is going to bust a gasket when she sees her precious Muffie," Hayley laughed behind her hand. I looked down at the once snowy-white Maltese, crinkling my nose at the smell coming off her. It was true. Dodge took a reluctant sniff, then a tentative lick of the greenish-brown muck. *Blech!* I knew dogs weren't picky eaters, but . . . ew!

I didn't know what I was going to say to Summer when we delivered Muffet in her compost suit. Worse than that, I suddenly didn't know what to say to Hayley. She'd acted so weird around Taylor that it was making *me* act weird around *her*.

"So, uh, where's Taylor?" I couldn't help asking when we got back to our bikes. If I sounded annoyed, she totally missed it.

"The dogs took off when you did, so he grabbed the burgers and went after them. I hope he can save them on his own!" She sighed and swung a leg over her bike.

*I'm surprised you didn't chase after* him! I thought, biting my tongue to keep the words from spilling out. I didn't want Hayley to be mad at me. I wasn't even sure why I was so mad at her. She'd just come to Muffet's rescue . . . and mine, too!

"Let's just take Muffet home to Mommy Dearest," I said, not that I was looking forward to *that* job. Using as few fingers as possible, I put the soiled pup in my bike basket.

Hayley snorted. "Maybe we can stick a note around her neck that says 'Wash Me' and leave her on the porch."

I half laughed — it might have been the best idea I'd heard all day — but Muffet looked a little hurt. She sat in the basket, shivering. "Sorry, Muff. I guess this is the price of your little afternoon adventure." Muffet's tail dropped lower but she kept her head held high.

Hayley and I didn't talk the rest of the ride to our neighborhood. The silence was weird. But I didn't want to think about it or talk about it, so I didn't say a thing. I just kept pedaling.

# CHAPTER 12

"Achoo!" I sneezed a big sneeze. It was so big I hit my nose on the sidewalk. *Bow-ow*. There was a smell in my snout that I wanted to get rid of. And it wasn't Muffet's rotten soup odor, either. That was actually kind of delicious. It was the tension smell between Hayley and my girl. It reminded me of the air before a rain — the smell of something about to happen. Of things that needed to be said.

I wished I could put my paw on the problem. I hadn't seen anything unusual. But neither girl was laughing. Or talking. Or petting me. In fact, Muffet was the only one in our little pack paying any attention to me at all.

She wagged and barked and threatened to leap out of Cassie's basket to get closer. Her gunk was starting to dry and fall off, but the smell hung on and I could tell Muffet was glad. That stench was like a badge. She'd earned it. Who'd want to put a pretty sweater on anydog who smelled like that? Actually, that might have been her motive.

As we got close to Hayley's house, Cassie finally spoke. "You don't have to come with us," she told her friend, staring at her handle bars. That wasn't what I expected her to say. It wasn't what Hayley expected, either.

Hayley's eyes seemed to shrink in her head. She was hurt. She opened her mouth, then closed it. Then opened it again. "Okay. I guess I should get home."

Cassie nodded and faked a smile. "Okay, I'll see you tomorrow."

I watched Hayley roll toward Spring Street. I watched her pedal away slowly, saw her look back over her shoulder. Once. Cassie didn't see, but I did. Hayley's brow crinkled. She almost called out, but didn't. Her tail tucked, she rode away.

"Dodge, come!"

As we turned onto Summer's street, Cassie started to breathe a little funny. When she hopped off to push her bike up the walk, Muffet jumped out of the basket and ran up the steps to bark at the Hills' door. I could tell Cassie wanted to run in the other direction, but she didn't. She was brave. I stood beside her. I was brave, too.

"Here goes," she mumbled as she pushed the doorbell. I heard footsteps, and the door opened. Summer looked at Cassie. Her eyes got skinny. She looked at me. Her lip pulled up on one side. She looked at Muffet and her mouth opened wide.

"What . . . did . . . you . . . *do?*" she demanded.

*Orowl.* There was a laughing bark that was jumping around in my throat. It was trying to get out. I told it to stay. *Stay!*

Cassie's mouth twitched. She told whatever was in her throat to stay, too.

Muffet wiggled like crazy and let out a yap. At least *she* was happy to see Summer.

Summer bent down, the sneer stuck on her face. When she got close enough for her human nose to catch a whiff, though, her sneer turned into a snarl. "Oh!" She stood up fast. "Oh my God. You stole my dog and you're returning her like this?" she shrieked, holding her nose. "What did you do to her?"

What? Stole her dog? Did something to her? "Woof!" I barked at that. No way. Little Miss Muffet followed *me*. And she worked hard at it, too.

Cassie stepped forward. Her paws were balled into fists. "I didn't steal your dog. I saved her. She was stuck in a Dumpster on the waterfront. And if it weren't for Dodge, she'd still be in there. So how about a little gratitude?"

Summer's snout wrinkled. "Gratitude? My Muffet would never let herself get this . . . filthy," she barked. She blinked her shiny eyes. The smell was really getting to her now. She stepped from foot to foot, and I nosed the muck-covered leash end. Summer saw the chewed stump and sucked in her breath. There it was. Proof. Muffet had chewed her way to freedom, but Summer wouldn't admit she'd been wrong. That girl didn't have half the pluck her dog had.

"I don't know why I'm surprised, Cassie," Summer howled. "You've always been a liar and a thief. I guess you get that from your mom. I read all about it in the paper, by the way — how she's off the force."

*Rrrrr.* Summer had stopped being funny. And I stopped telling the noises in my throat to stay. "Grrrr." My growl rumbled in my throat. Cassie pet it back. She told me to cool it without saying a word. I listened, but it wasn't easy.

"Whatever," Cassie mumbled. "Come on, Dodge, she's not worth it." Waving her hand, she stepped off the stoop. She walked in a hurry to where she'd parked her bike. She was done here, and so was I.

"Yiiiip!" Muffet barked her thanks to me.

The small dog was in for a bath full of perfume. I was sure of that. But her bark told me she thought it had been totally worth it. And that she was grateful for our help. *Woof!* At least one of those girls knew how to behave.

# CHAPTER 13

I turned quickly and stomped off of Summer Hill's porch. Dodge gave a final "woof," and I was grateful Summer didn't get the last word. I hated everything about Summer. Her matchy-matchy outfits. Her smug smile. Her ability to get to me. Everything!

Summer Hill. More like Summer *Pill*.

I must have been grumbling to myself as I put my bike away, because Dodge nosed my palm. I drew a deep breath and let it out in a whoosh. "I know," I said. "I should just ignore her. It's just . . ." It was just everything. Mom getting suspended. Hayley getting all gaga over Taylor. And Summer being Summer. It was just too much.

Before Mom got suspended, I looked forward to coming home at the end of the day. Downtime. Flop time. Relax time. Not anymore. As soon as we walked through the door a smell about as appetizing as Muffet's vegetable muck accosted me. Mom was in the kitchen, and Owen was setting the table for four. He gave me a look. "Where's Dad?" I asked quietly, so Mom wouldn't hear. Owen raised his eyebrows, which meant, "Your guess is as good as mine."

"Great," I mumbled. Things were definitely getting worse if Dad wasn't even coming home for meals. I felt a little mad at him for staying away from home — it didn't feel fair. Then I walked into the kitchen and thought maybe he had the right idea. Maybe I was just jealous.

The counter was covered in half-empty condiment jars and Tupperware containers, and the bad smell was coming from the stove. Mom was obviously trying to use up stuff in the fridge.

"Hi, Mom. Need any help?" I asked, hoping for a no. I scraped the bottom of the pot on the stove, wondering what the residue was.

"No. I've put together a shepherd's pie," she said, opening the oven. "Dad took a double shift. It's just the four of us tonight, so I improvised." Mom's smile was slapped on and didn't hide her stress, or the bags under her eyes. Just like the bottle of ketchup wasn't going to hide the funky flavor of her improvised dinner.

Mom carried the steaming dish of "pie" to the table, and we all sat down. Sam made a face.

"It's not that bad," Mom said tiredly. "Try it."

I took a bite and washed it down with a long drink of milk, but Sam made the mistake of chewing. If things weren't so terrible I might have enjoyed seeing her gag. But I didn't. Dad's empty chair made dinner seem lonely. It was a reminder that my parents weren't getting along and also made me think of Uncle Mark, whose empty spot could never be filled. I swallowed hard and took another sip of milk.

Under the table, Dodge's head rested on my feet, like always. I dropped a little food for him, but he barely bothered to eat it. The weight of his big head let me know he was feeling like the rest of us: miserable.

"Earbuds out, Owen," Mom said. Usually this would get a major eye roll from my big brother, but he didn't even protest as he put the little headphones away. He just sat and stared.

On the other side of the table, which somehow seemed like the other side of the world, Sam was talking a mile a minute. She went on and on about Girls' Rock Camp, ignoring everyone else's misery. "Did you register me online yet, Mom?" she demanded. "It's only a thousand dollars for two weeks."

"What a bargain," Owen mumbled.

I rolled my eyes. How could Sam be so clueless? If we had a thousand dollars for Girls' Rock Camp, would we really be eating icky leftovers? Then I noticed Mom's face and decided to change the subject.

"Hey, Mom, you know GreenWay? That company that owns a bunch of warehouses on the waterfront?"

Mom nodded but didn't say anything.

"Is that the company putting in the new park and estuary?" The question had been fluttering around the back of my brain ever since we met Mr. Albrici. His comment about everything being bought up reminded me of the GreenWay signs that Hayley and I had noticed. I wondered if they were the people buying . . . and pressuring Mr. Albrici to sell. But why would they want to buy property that was supposed to be turned into a park? Were they in charge of building it?

"I don't think so, honey," Mom said. "The city is in charge of that." Her eyebrows twitched, though, and the line between them appeared. I could almost see the gears in her brain engaging. She knew more than she was saying, which meant (1) I was probably onto something, and (2) those gears still moved. Excellent!

"So the city will buy the property from current owners and then put in the park? I thought they'd be starting by now," I said to my plate of awful. "They made such a big deal about it."

Mom nodded again but didn't say anything as she absentmindedly forked up a bite of food. I could tell she was thinking. Mulling something over.

Feeling a little lighter, I pushed back my chair and started to clear. Cleanup was going to take a while. Luckily

I had Dodge. He took one for the team and swabbed away the shepherd's pie with his wide, pink tongue, prepping the plates for the dishwasher. "You're a miracle," I told him, pausing long enough to stroke his smooth ears.

When we finally finished, we headed into the office. I "needed" some paper. And I also wanted to take another look at Mom's file. I pulled several sheets of lined paper out of a drawer while I scanned the desktop. Right away I spotted the manila folder sticking out from under a stack of papers, and something else: a blue folder I was pretty sure hadn't been there before. I pulled the blue one out. It was labeled "Corps," too, but was thinner than the other one. And underneath "Corps" someone had scribbled the word "unofficial."

My heart started to thud. I looked at Dodge, the open office door, and back at the blue folder. Dodge padded to the door to keep watch. My hands trembled and I slid several documents out. I scanned each page as quickly as I could, my eyes zeroing in on words like "raid" and "search" and "seizure."

"This'll need a thorough reading," I whispered to

Dodge. These "unofficial" papers would probably be way more informative than Mom's police file. I was about to shove the whole thing under my shirt when Dodge made a sound in his throat. Uh-oh. Time was up. I barely managed to cram the blue folder back under a pile of papers on the desk before Mom walked in.

"Oh, Cassie, I didn't know you were in here," she said.

"I was just getting some paper," I mumbled. I hoped she wouldn't notice my blazing cheeks. Luckily, she wasn't looking. She was focused on the desk. I just stared as she lifted the whole pile, taking all the folders and my hopes of reading more anytime soon.

"Be sure to turn off the lights when you leave, okay?"

I nodded mutely, feeling guilty and disappointed. My fingerprints were all over the blue card stock — totally incriminating — but I hadn't had enough time to glean any real clues.

I was so busy being bummed out that I almost missed the small slip of paper that fluttered out of the blue folder as Mom left the room. I waited until she was all the way up the stairs before bending down to retrieve it. I glanced at the note and a shudder went up my spine. It was a piece of paper from a desk tablet. On it was a handwritten note. I recognized the handwriting immediately — I'd seen it on birthday cards and homemade treasure maps.

I was looking at a note from Uncle Mark.

# CHAPTER 14

The Mom was going bonkers. Pulling everything out of the closets. *Everything.* She went from sitting at the kitchen table drinking coffee to making piles all over the house. Clothes, books, toys, sports stuff, gadgets, and a mountain of old T-shirts and towels for Pet Rescue, to make the beds cozier. I wanted to bury myself in that heap of cotton. Hide from The Mom's madness. But I knew she'd shoo me out of there in a heartbeat. There was no escape. Aw, *woof.*

I padded up the stairs and eyed The Cat, who snoozed on the windowsill. In the sun. Out of the way. It was totally unfair, how easy it was for cats to get out of the way. Much harder for a big German shepherd. With a disgruntled yawn and a stretch, I chose a corner by the stairs to curl up in. I'd just have to wait it out.

Lately I'd been doing a lot of waiting, which I hated. I especially hated waiting without napping. The Mom made a lot of noise while she worked. Talked to herself. Listened to the radio. And worse, ran the vacuum. I hated the vacuum. It could not be trusted. It could not be approached. And it was impossible to ignore.

I stood up. Circled. Lay down again. I scratched some itchy spots. Licked some fur. Found some bits of Muffet's compost stew in my coat and chewed them out. Nothing helped.

The vacuum stopped, and The Mom came into the hall with an armful of books. Mumbling. She dumped them into a box and went back into her bedroom. The Cat yawned and stretched. Lazy beast. Finally the house got quiet. Thank goodness. All this purging put a dog on edge. Even a dog with special training. I put my head on my paws. I e-x-h-a-l-e-d and closed my eyes.

*Tha-woomp, tha-woomp, tha-woomp.* I ran through a grassy field, chasing butterflies. Crickets cricked. Birds sang. Somebody cried. Wait, cried? That wasn't right. I stopped running and looked around, confused. Who was crying? It sounded like a human, but there were no humans in my field — just grasses, wildflowers, and butterflies. Then I got it. The field was a dream. The crying was coming from the awake world. My legs twitched. I wanted to chase butterflies. But I had to wake up. Get up. Provide comfort. It was part of my job.

I bounded over one last patch of dream daisies and forced my eyes open. I lurched to my feet and trotted toward the crying noise. I was barely awake, but my good ear pricked painfully. And what I saw made my tail touch the floor.

The Mom sat on her bed. Her hands covered her face. She rocked back and forth, and sobbed. An open book sat next to her on the bed, but not a regular book. This was the kind humans wrote in. A diary. I pulled the box of tissues off the dresser and carried them to the bed. Tissues were good for humans when their eyes got leaky. I put my nose on her knee.

The Mom didn't look at me, but she knew I was there. And I knew it helped, a little. I sat close to her. Finally she patted my head. "Oh, Dodge," she sniffled. "What have I done? It's all such a mess." She smelled like saltwater, and her face was blotchy. "How are we going to get out of this?" I licked her cheek and puffed air out through my nose. I was good at cleaning up messes. But not this kind.

We sat and stayed, together, for a long time. Really long. We were still staying when the doorbell rang. My ear twitched, but The Mom didn't move. "What now?" she asked quietly. Then, all of a sudden, she was on her feet. She checked her face in the mirror and smoothed her sweater.

I trotted down the stairs in front of her, barking out my greeting. Who was there? I sniffed the crack around the edges of the door. A dog could smell a lot around the edges. I smelled onions and . . . steak?

"It's all right, Dodge," The Mom told me as she opened the door. But I wasn't so sure.

When she saw the person on the stoop, her mouth dropped open. More than a little. "Mayor Baudry," she said, straightening and holding the door wide. The mayor was not my favorite human — he liked to be in charge too much. And he wasn't very good at it. But he was holding a doggie bag. A doggie bag full of steak. "I just came from a lunch meeting," he said, shaking the bag slightly. The smell of grilled meat drifted right to my nose. It made my tail thump on the floor. Steak. I loved steak. Steak was my favorite.

"Can the old boy have the leftovers?" the mayor asked. He meant me. The steak was for me! The Mom smiled and nodded. I licked my chops. Mayor Baudry opened the bag and dropped a hefty piece of steak — rare, the way I like it! — onto the tile floor. *Mmm, steak!*

While I gobbled, they talked. "I'm so sorry about all this, Dorrie," the mayor said. "I tried my best to stop the investigation, but my hands were tied." I glanced up. His hands didn't *look* tied.

"Yes, I'm sure," The Mom agreed as she led him into the living room. I stayed with the steak.

"I just came by to tell you that I'm doing absolutely everything I can to expedite this terrible process," he continued. "Bellport needs its police chief at work, protecting its citizens!"

I half listened while I licked meat juice from the floor. The taste of steak lingered on the tile and my tongue.

"I really appreciate it. This has been quite stressful, as you might imagine," The Mom said. I licked until the flavor was gone. I wished there was more. I also wished The Mom would stop talking and tell the mayor to go home. He was useless. And she was acting more Beta than Alpha. It wasn't like her. It wasn't right. She was The Chief! Top dog! Alpha all the way!

I silently told her to sit straight and stick her ears up. Be strong! But she couldn't feel what I was thinking the way Cassie could. And The Chief I used to report to had been gobbled up by guilt. And fear. And sadness. *Grrrr.* Guilt and fear were the enemy. I took a final lick and went to stand by The Mom. Never thought I'd say it, but The Chief needed backup. Big-time.

# CHAPTER 15

I propped my history text up on my desk and slouched in my seat. I was in the back row but still needed to be as incognito as possible. I wasn't paying attention at all, at least not to Ms. Diamond's lecture on the Mayas. I had my own history to deal with — family history — and it was traumatic.

The note I'd found the night before and the pages I'd copied from Mom's file sat on the desk in front of me. The note, in particular, was freaking me out. Just the handwriting was creepy — it felt like reading a letter from a ghost. I didn't totally get the meaning of what

Uncle Mark had written, either. But then I wasn't sure I wanted to.

**D —**

I'm not waiting — the paperwork will take too long. They know we're onto them and we don't have much time, so I'm doing this on my own. Without a paper trail they won't be able to blame you. Please don't be mad — what I find will break this thing wide open. I've been connecting the dots. It's all there. The corruption, participation, everything. But I have to act now. I'm writing this note in case I get into trouble, but Dodge has my back. I'll be fine. So, now you know what I'm up to, and soon I'll know exactly what we're up against.

**— M**

The initials and the handwriting and the mention of Dodge made it clear — it was a note from Uncle Mark to Mom. He was telling her that he wasn't going to wait to do something, something that required paperwork. . . . Was he talking about a search warrant? Was he doing something illegal? That would explain why the note fell out of the "unofficial" file. What had Uncle Mark and Mom gotten themselves into?

Feeling miserable, I glanced up at Ms. Diamond's scrawl on the board, then down at the next sheet of paper from Mom's file. It was a copy of a newspaper article about The Corps.

**The Bellport Police Department continues its investigation of The Corps, an association it believes may be responsible for a significant percentage of Bellport crime, including drug dealing, gambling, extortion, and money laundering. "I believe that if The Corps is involved in illegal activities, it needs to be brought to justice," stated Mayor Morris Baudry.**

**But others in the community are not convinced of The Corps's involvement in crime. Well-known local businessman William Kemper touted the long-standing philanthropy of the group. "The Corps has done more for Bellport than any other organization," he stated. "It is never wise to bite the hand that feeds you."**

I stared at the page, the name William Kemper ringing a bell in my head. I looked over a few of the copies I'd made from Mom's police file and found him. William Kemper, GreenWay executive. He was the guy at the ribbon-cutting ceremony with the mayor. And somebody, maybe Uncle Mark, had pointed out that Slatterly was in that photo, too.

Mom and Uncle Mark had obviously been gathering evidence to indict members of The Corps. But was GreenWay connected somehow?

I leaned over the papers on my desk and rubbed my temples. Trying to sort all this out made my head hurt.

I was still staring down at my notebook when the bell rang for lunch. My stomach in knots, I got to my feet, wishing I could sit there and think for another hour. For one thing, the pieces of the puzzle hadn't clicked in to place. For another, I wasn't looking forward to seeing Hayley.

Oh boy. Hayley. We hadn't talked since the Dumpster incident . . . two whole days. Under normal circumstances that would have been about six phone calls, twenty-two texts, and who knows how many face-to-face conversations.

I sighed miserably. Nothing about my life was normal right now. Not even my relationship with my best human friend.

I got to my feet and shoved the papers in my backpack. Maybe I could skip lunch. Or eat in the bathroom. It couldn't be that hard to avoid one person, could it?

I was keeping my eyes peeled in the hall when Alicia pounced. "You have to talk," she announced, pulling me into a corner where Hayley was standing, staring nervously at her shoes. "You are my only friends at this school. Heck, you are my only friends in this country. On this continent! So whatever is going on between you? You need to work it out."

I couldn't help but admire Alicia's directness. Plus, she was right. It was totally stupid not to talk to Hayley . . . about anything. Only I wasn't prepared to talk to her. I didn't even know what to say. Then I remembered that this was Hayley Gault, champion talker. She'd probably do enough talking for both of us. Which was good, because I was too freaked out about this stuff with Uncle Mark to form a coherent thought.

I looked up at Hayley's dark eyes and saw the worry right away. Her forehead was all bunched up. "I know it's weird," she started.

I waited.

"The thing with Taylor."

I waited a little more.

"I mean, that I think he's cute and everything." Her eyebrows dropped. "But why didn't you tell me how adorable he is?"

"Adorable?" My mouth dropped open. "Hayley, he's not a puppy!"

"I know. But —"

"And he's way too old for you! He's the same age as Owen!"

Hayley bit her lip nervously. "I know that, of course," she admitted. "But . . ." A dreamy, spaced-out look overtook her face, and I rolled my eyes. She was going totally bonkers about too-old-for-her Taylor all over again, and he wasn't even in the building!

# CHAPTER 16

The door closed behind the mayor, and The Mom let out a big sigh. A tired sigh. A Beta sigh. "Woof!" I told her. Head up! Tail up! But she didn't seem to get the message. She just gave me an absentminded pat and walked into the kitchen. I followed. Good stuff happened in the kitchen.

I was still behind the counter when I heard the fridge door open. *Click, click, click, click.* I trotted across the tile floor and sat down, looking very patient. And hungry. But not beggy. The Mom did not go for beggy. Or whiny. Ever.

She didn't seem to notice me not begging. But I was patient. I watched as she pulled a bunch of stuff out of the fridge. More than sandwich makings. Way more. "This needs a good cleaning," she mumbled as she unearthed a stack of Tupperware. Some of it smelled like last night's shepherd's pie. Not her best work, but I wasn't a picky eater. I was just an eater.

The Mom kept pulling things out of the fridge. My nose quivered. My mouth watered. I forced my butt to stay still on the floor. Within minutes the counters were covered. Plastic containers, jars, bottles, and bags. And the food inside them! I might have whined. Just a little. Luckily, The Mom didn't hear it. And I admit I drooled. More than a little. Cleaning out the fridge was way better than organizing closets! And we were getting to the good part.

"Hungry, Dodge?" The Mom finally asked as she opened the lid on a container of old rice and beans. Too old for humans, but not too old for a dog! She scooped them into my bowl and I lapped them up. Lunchtime!

While I ate, she tossed out a bunch of old condiments. I didn't really care about condiments. They were fine on sandwiches and burgers but nothing amazing on their own. Nothing to bark about. Except maybe mayo. Mayo was special. Then I saw it. The mother lode. A hefty block of stinky cheese. Cheese! I loved cheese! Cheese was my favorite.

"I think this is for you, too," The Mom said. She dropped it into my dish. Delicious! I licked the outside. I sank my teeth in. I chewed. So smelly. So creamy. So good! *Slow down!* I told myself. *Savor it!* Those were Cassie's words. But I could not eat slow. Not cheese. Not ever. Before I knew it, the chunk was gone.

I was licking the bits off my whiskers when The Cat strolled in. Ha! She was too late. All that was left were slimy vegetables and spoiled milk. I licked my chops, extra slow, so The Cat wouldn't miss it. The only thing better than a midday meal was getting to rub it in.

The Cat stalked out. I licked my bowl clean, again. Then I sat down and watched The Mom, who was busy. Busy cleaning up the mess from cleaning out the fridge.

When all the food containers were washed or tossed, The Mom wiped down the counters. Three times. No stray crumbs allowed. Then she wrung out the dishrag. She folded it. She draped it over the faucet so the sides lined up perfectly. I just stared.

"Well, that's done," she said. "Now we can get back to work upstairs." The cheese began to rumble in my stomach. I wanted to have a postlunch snooze on the couch, to digest while I waited for Cassie. But I was a trained dog. I put duty first. And I knew that looking after The Mom was my top priority. Where she went, I went.

Upstairs, The Mom marched straight into her room and tossed the book that made her cry into the garbage can. "Enough is enough," she told me. I didn't exactly understand what she meant. Enough what? But I *did* know the book was important. Maybe full of clues! I had to get it out of the trash. When nobody was looking.

I sat down at the foot of the bed. I put on my innocent face. I kept my eyes locked on the garbage can while The Mom sorted books on a shelf. Finally she left the room with a boxful. As she disappeared down the stairs, I slunk up to the can. I put a paw on the rim and tipped it. Crouching low, I stuck my nose in. Earwax. Candy. Phlegm. I nosed past the tissues and wrappers and grabbed the book with my teeth. Not too firmly — only enough to hang on to it and not leave marks. Just the right bite.

Getting out was trickier. When I backed up, the trash can came with me. Uh-oh. I was stuck! I stood up on all fours and shook my head. I wasn't just stuck. I was really stuck. And I couldn't see a thing!

I backed up and hit a wall. So much for stealth. I threw my head from side to side, hard. Again. And again. And again. *Thwack!* The wastebasket flew off and hit The Dad's dresser. Scraps of paper and tissue flew everywhere. The diary slid under the bed. *Oh, woof.*

I was surveying the damage when The Cat strolled into the bedroom, looking around. Smug. I ignored her and got to work. I nosed the trash can upright. I gathered some tissues and papers and put them back in the can. The tissues were tricky — they stuck to my mouth. I was trying to shake them off when I heard The Mom coming up the stairs. I moved fast, but The Mom moved faster. When she walked in, I still had a tissue in my mouth. I had no choice. I sat down at the foot of the bed and swallowed the dry wad. It wasn't half as good as the block of cheese.

From the windowsill, The Cat rumbled. She was laughing. I swallowed some more, trying to get the dry bits down my throat. I put my head on my paws and looked at the book under the bed. My shoulders slumped with disappointment. My work here was unfinished.

# CHAPTER 17

"So. Study session at my house?" Hayley asked as we pushed out the Harbor Middle doors. "I've got some killer red velvet cupcakes. And I promise I won't say a word about what's-his-name." Her eyes were bright, and I could tell she wasn't teasing or trying to upset me. And just thinking about her red velvets made my mouth water.

"Cream cheese frosting?"

Hayley squinted, totally offended. "Cream cheese? No way. That'd be totally pedestrian. Crème fraîche."

Mmm, crème fraîche. Now my mouth was *really* watering. "I'd love to, but I can't. I've got to get home and spring Dodge. Mom's been driving all of us nuts with her cleaning, and she doesn't let him get away with *anything*."

"Harsh," Hayley said, nodding. She'd seen Mom in action plenty of times, so she understood. But she had a weird, hesitant look on her face, too. "Can I, um, come over?" she ventured.

I immediately spotted an opportunity and donned a serious expression. "For three red velvets with extra —"

Hayley held out her hand, cutting me off. "Deal. I can make the delivery tomorrow."

I grinned, letting her know I'd have let her come even *without* the red velvets. Boy crazy or not, she was still the best thing on two legs.

It didn't take us long to get home on our bikes, and Dodge met us as we walked in. Dodge always met me at the door, but this time he looked like he had something to tell me. Something more than "I'm sooooo happy to see you." He also barely acknowledged Hayley, which was strange. Dodge loved Hayley and practically frisked her for treats whenever he saw her.

"Do you think he's mad that I didn't bring him anything?" she asked, looking worried.

I shook my head and crouched down, trying to read his face. "What's up, Dodge? Want to go out?" He let out a yowl, hopping a little on all fours. That sounded like a yes. Who wouldn't want to stretch their legs after being cooped up all day? I opened the door, but he just stood there. Then he barked and stepped back. Dodge didn't want to go outside.

"Okaaay." I closed the door, confused.

"Weird," Hayley pronounced.

"Totally." I watched my dog walk toward the stairs and stop at the bottom, a clear signal to follow. Well, all right. "Come on," I said to Hayley. I expected Dodge to go straight to our room, but he plopped himself down by my parents' door instead.

"Weirder," Hayley mumbled.

"Totally."

We were standing there staring at Dodge when Mom peeked her head out of the hall linen closet. "Oh, hi, honey. Hi, Hayley," she greeted us, her voice muffled behind the giant pile of sheets she was carrying. I spotted an ancient Barbie Princess set and was glad she was finally getting rid of them.

"You need some help, Mrs. Sullivan?" Hayley offered, stepping forward before I could stop her.

"That would be terrific," Mom replied. "Did you hear that, Cassie? Your friend Hayley *offered* to help."

I made a face while Hayley unloaded half the pile from Mom's arms and followed her down the stairs. *Great*, I thought. Not only was Hayley gaga for Taylor, she'd decided to become my mom's helper, too. Next thing I knew she'd be doing makeovers with Sam.

But I didn't have long to ponder the horrors of that, because as soon as they were gone, Dodge dashed into my parents' bedroom and stuck his snout under their bed. Dropping his belly to the ground, he wriggled forward, grunting softly.

"What are you after?" I asked, getting on my knees and lifting the bed skirt. I saw it right away — a book of some kind that Dodge couldn't reach. I quickly shimmied under the bed and grabbed it, emerging just as Mom and Hayley came up the stairs. By the time I was back on my feet, Dodge was practically standing on top of me, blocking the book from view. It didn't take a detective to get the message. The book was contraband.

"We're gonna do homework in my room," I told Mom, hiding the smuggled goods behind my back. Dodge covered me as I exited awkwardly, ignoring the look Hayley shot in my direction. I beelined it to my room and closed the door.

"Did I just witness a covert operation?" Hayley asked, unable to keep the excitement out of her voice.

"I think so," I replied with a laugh. "You may even have aided and abetted." I pulled the book from behind my back, and the laugh died in my throat. I was holding Mom's diary. I stared for a second before cracking it open and seeing that the first entry was dated September 24. Over a year ago — three days after Uncle Mark was killed.

"Oh my goodness," I gasped, snapping the book closed and sitting down on my bed. I was afraid to read. To look. I felt guilty for even considering it! And at the same time, I knew I probably held the answer to Mom's suspension mystery and Uncle Mark's death in my hands. Or at least part of it.

"What is it?" Hayley asked.

"My mom's diary," I added in a hoarse whisper.

Dodge whimpered and came over to rest his head on

my lap. I patted him. He'd done a good job. This was key info. But . . .

Hayley got it. She walked over and took the diary out of my hands, eyeing it like the stolen property it was.

I felt sick. "I can't read it." Respect for privacy was a theme in our house of five. Reading Mom's diary crossed a line for sure, not to mention how reading it would *feel*.

"You don't have to," Hayley assured me. She exhaled slowly. "I will. That way if your mom asks if you read her diary, you can honestly say no."

I squinted at her, confused.

"I'll just happen to read out loud, and you can just happen to hear it." She smiled slyly, and I felt my head nod. It was sneaky. It was bold. And I was all in.

Hayley opened the book to the first entry and took a deep breath. "'I almost wish it had been me,'" she read quietly, her voice filling the room. "'That I had been the one who died. If it weren't for Joe and the kids, I couldn't live with Mark's pointless death at all. . . .'" She trailed off and looked up at me, her eyes full of worry. "Are we sure we want to do this?"

I wasn't the slightest bit sure. But I knew that I had to do whatever I could to help my family, because we were in crisis all over again. We were falling apart. I nodded my head.

"'I said so many terrible things to him,'" Hayley continued, "'so many things I regret. I was fixated on the fact that he was breaking protocol. I was furious he didn't tell me to my face. I was mad he wrote it all in a note. But who could blame him? He knew how I'd react. The raid was supposed to go off with a full team, and Mark went in alone of his own accord. It was so dangerous. I was so angry. But he did it to protect me. For Joe and the kids. I didn't want to admit that I might need protecting, but I did. Only I also needed to protect *him*. All I can do now is protect his memory, his reputation. I can change history — make it look like he was following my orders. If only it would bring him back.'"

I stopped listening for a second, because my brain was too overwhelmed to keep up. Mom and Mark must have gotten into a huge fight over that note. She said she was mad. Their last words to each other had been words of anger. . . .

" 'I can't tell anyone what I'm going to do. Not even Joe. I feel terrible for the lies I'm about to tell, but Joe is already in agony. He'd fall apart if he knew that Mark's stubbornness ended his life, that his own wife could have stopped it, should have stopped it, and didn't. . . .' "

# CHAPTER 18

"Are you sure you don't want me to stay?" I heard Hayley ask. *Yes. Stay, Hayley.* She'd stayed for dinner, sitting in The Dad's seat. And after that, she'd read Cassie more of the book. Finally, the reading was done. At least for tonight. *Woof.* Listening to those terrible words made my head hurt. So did watching Cassie's face. Her eyes leaked. Her face twisted. She looked like she'd been kicked. Over and over.

I leaned into Cassie, nuzzling her and licking tears away. "No, that's okay," Cassie said as she stroked my bad ear. "You should go. Dodge and I are just going to go to sleep."

Hayley looked at us. She smelled like doubt.

"I'm fine," Cassie said, trying to smile. But her mouth curled up like she was growling.

I looked at Hayley. She didn't believe it. I didn't believe it, either. Cassie wasn't fine. That book made her feel terrible. Maybe I should have left it in the trash. Maybe it belonged there.

"Go!" Cassie barked impatiently. She was tired. And grumpy. "Really."

"All right," Hayley said quietly. She set the book down on Cassie's desk. "I'll see you in the morning."

Cassie sighed. "Thanks," she said. "Thanks for your help."

Hayley squeezed my girl's shoulder. "Anytime," she said.

Cassie hid the book in a dresser drawer, put on her pajamas, and crawled into bed. I pulled Bunny out, circled, and settled in with a *whump*. Cassie's hand fell into my fur. I chewed Bunny's ear and waited for her to fall asleep.

It took longer than ever. When Cassie's breathing finally changed, I tucked Bunny in. I licked the salt off Cassie's cheeks and padded downstairs. I was really looking forward to getting out. Stretching my legs. Making my rounds. It had been too long.

My nose was quivering. Ready. Then I saw The Dad at the fridge. Just standing. And staring. This wasn't suspicious. I'd seen it before. He did it when he couldn't sleep. But it meant no rounds for now.

"Hey, Dodger," The Dad said as he closed the food box. He ruffled my fur with one hand and fed me a piece of salami with the other. *Mmm, salami.* I loved salami. Salami was my favorite. The Dad loved salami, too, but not right now. Right now he didn't love anything. He slumped at the counter. "I just don't get it," he said. "What is she hiding? Why is she hiding anything? I'm supposed to be her partner. . . ." He trailed off and stared into space. He looked like Bunny — unstuffed.

Then, all of a sudden, he got up and left the kitchen. He headed for the stairs. Stopped. Changed his mind. Walked over to the closet. He pulled out a blanket and a pillow from the top shelf. This *was* suspicious. I'd never seen it before. The Dad always slept in his den with The Mom.

He spread the blanket over the couch. I whimpered. "Don't tell," he said. He crawled under the blanket and closed his eyes. I circled and dropped. Settled on the floor. Just for a while.

It took The Dad a really, really long time to fall asleep. Even longer than Cassie.

# CHAPTER 19

I woke with a jolt and sat up, panicked. I'd had a bad dream. A *terrible* dream. I'd been riding all over town in a patrol car, reading Mom's diary over the loud-speaker — broadcasting secrets as the cruiser rolled down the street. The looks on the faces of the citizens of Bellport were horrible: disappointment, betrayal, disgust. And then there was Summer Hill's expression: sheer delight.

I felt a hint of relief when Dodge's ears and snout appeared over the edge of the bed, and the rest of his head followed. His eyes asked if I was okay. I patted him in response.

*It was a dream*, I told myself, shivering. At least the worst part anyway. It was barely light out, but trying to go back to sleep after my nightmare was pointless. I pulled on some clothes in the semidark, wondering if I could act normal around my family at breakfast. Making it through dinner had been really hard, and I'd had Dodge *and* Hayley there for backup. I wasn't sure I could make it through another meal. I needed to make a quick break. Get out before I got caught up.

"I think I'm gonna head out early," I told Dodge as we left our room. He lowered his eyebrows at me, which I tried hard to ignore. I didn't need to add more guilt to my already heaping pile.

In the kitchen, I scooped kibble into Dodge's bowl, giving him a little extra. Then I quickly scrawled a note to Mom. I was grabbing a banana when Owen ambled up from downstairs. So much for a clean break.

"You're up early," he yawned in my direction.

"Or late, depending on how you look at it. I haven't been exactly sleeping lately," I admitted.

Owen nodded. "Me, either." He stood there in the kitchen, looking bleary and disheartened. "It's gonna be okay, though, right?" He stroked the top of Dodge's head.

I gaped at him in surprise. He was asking me? What did I know? Dodge gave me a sad chocolate stare, and I smiled weakly at both of them. "I sure hope so."

Owen half nodded, then shuffled forward and opened his arms. Biting my lip, I stepped into them. Into a hug. We stood there for a few seconds in the kitchen, hugging, with Dodge nosing our legs. I couldn't remember the last time Owen and I had hugged, and I felt myself tearing up. But I couldn't cry. I had stuff to do. Besides, Mom could've walked in at any second.

The thought of seeing Mom made me pull away harder than I meant to, and Owen looked a little hurt. "I've got to head out," I explained. "See you later?"

Owen shrugged, back to his teenager self, and opened the cereal cupboard. "Sure." I gave Dodge a kiss good-bye. Luckily Owen dropped a few flakes of cereal on the floor, which distracted him while I left.

Outside, I tried to breathe and shake off all the family stuff I'd been carrying around, the way Dodge shook off water. But it was on me good, and I felt extra heavy as I got on my bike and started for school.

"I'm coming with you," Hayley announced when classes were over. "No ifs, ands, or buts."

I nodded as we walked down the school steps with Alicia. Hayley walked close, our shoulders practically touching. "You didn't read the diary," she reminded me quietly, her dark eyes full of empathy. "I did."

"Yeah, but I know what it says," I reminded her. "That's almost as bad."

Alicia put a hand on my arm when we got to the sidewalk. "I'm so sorry. About everything," she said. "Is there anything I can do?"

"Got a magic wand?" I asked hopefully.

"You're going to get through this," Hayley insisted. "Chin up. Let's head to the waterfront. The pups are waiting."

"Pups?" Alicia asked. "What pups?"

"Some strays in the warehouse district," Hayley explained. "Cassie and Taylor have been trying to rescue them."

"Oh, the poor things!" Alicia cried. "I hope they

weren't mistreated like my Hugo was." She shuddered. "He's such a marshmallow. I can't imagine what happened to him before . . ."

"You want to come with us?" I asked.

Alicia looked at her mom's station wagon pulling up to the curb. "Can't. Orthodontist appointment. See you tomorrow!"

We waved good-bye and hopped on our bikes, pedaling for home. We picked up Dodge, then burgers, and rode to the waterfront. Taylor was already at our spot with the crates. "They're still here," he confirmed as we parked our bikes. "But there's no way I can get them out without you, Cassie."

"You mean the burgers," I replied, wagging the bag in the air before setting them down.

"No, I mean you," Taylor insisted. "I mean Cassandra Sullivan: Dog Magician." Taylor's gushing made me smile, just a little. "The dogs and I would be lost without her," he confided to Hayley.

"I know *exactly* what you mean." Hayley's goofy grin made me remember how lucky I was to have friends like Taylor and Hayley and Dodge. I was the one who'd be lost without them.

Feeling a little more like myself, I reached for a burger. Only my hand closed on nothing. The bag was gone!

"Dodge, again?" Taylor said accusingly.

Dodge was wandering nearby sniffing, tail down, like he felt bad. But it wasn't like him to steal food — especially the burgers. He knew what they were for, and that he always got at least one of his own. Plus this was the second time the whole bag had disappeared, paper and all. It didn't add up.

"Dodge? You okay?" I asked as I gave him a scratch. He wasn't acting guilty, but did seem . . . off. Distracted. And now we were out of bait.

"I could head back to the Smokehouse for more," I offered.

Hayley dug around in her backpack and pulled out a batch of peanut butter bars sprinkled with caramelized bacon. "Do you think these would work?"

I got a peanut buttery bacony noseful and smiled. Dodge looked up from his wandering and licked his chops. Would they ever! The strays under the docks had probably been living off trash since they were puppies, and those bars smelled amazing. Hayley had mad baking skills — only a robot would be able to resist her treats. "They'll work, all right," I whooped as Taylor sat down to pull off his boots.

Three minutes later I was crawling under the loading dock, carefully cradling Hayley's bars in my hand.

Up ahead, I saw something in the darkness. The glint of eyes. A stray pup! "It's okay," I told him — or her. "I'm not going to hurt you. I have a treat. . . ." I held out a bar and a sloppy mouth gobbled it up. That was fast!

"Good dog," I said in a soothing voice. "Now, where's your friend?" I heard a whimper and felt a nose. Maybe the chow hound would follow me out from under the dock. Reaching for another bar, I scooted backward, luring him. The dog's paws scraped along the ground. He was coming!

When we got to the edge of the dock, I squinted in the light and looked for the pup, expecting to have to encourage him the rest of the way out. Instead a large English bull terrier climbed right into my lap and scarfed down the other bar!

"Well, hello!" I said, getting a hand on his scruff. This wasn't one of the timid black-and-white strays we'd been trying to catch. This guy wasn't scrawny or shy at all. In fact, he was a little chubby . . . like maybe he'd been eating bags full of burgers! He gave me a friendly slurp. "I think we found our thief!" I told Hayley and Taylor. "This guy has some serious burger breath."

"Oh my gosh," Hayley exclaimed, squatting. "Look at him!" The terrier pooch scrambled out of my lap and into Hayley's. He licked her face again and again, like he knew she'd made the bars and wanted to thank her personally. Taylor clipped a collar around the dog's neck while he climbed all over Hayley. When Hayley stood up and he couldn't reach her face, he hopped up beside her and licked her knees!

"I don't think we need a crate for this guy," Taylor said, laughing. "He'd follow Hayley anywhere!"

I had to agree. Hayley definitely had a new four-legged friend. A smile spread across my face as I watched the two of them. The burger burglar was a total sweetie pie! I looked around for Dodge — he'd probably want to meet the burger thief — but didn't see his brown tail anywhere. "Dodge?" I called. "Dooodge?" No answer. Dog gone!

# CHAPTER 20

I knew I should stay. Cassie told me to, and I was trained. My head said: Sit. But my body said: Move it.

Maybe it was because I'd been fooled by the Burger Burglar again. Maybe it was because I'd been in the house too much lately. Or maybe it was instinct.

Whatever it was, I needed to sniff some stuff out. I got to my feet. S-t-r-e-t-c-h-e-d. Shook. S-t-r-e-t-c-h-e-d again, and padded silently away from the loading dock.

The pavement around the waterfront was in bad shape. The buildings weren't much better. I passed several abandoned warehouses. Then Muffet's Dumpster. I wondered if the spunky pup had any of the garbagey smell left on her and licked my chops.

My mind wandered as I sniffed. Seaweed. Oil. Bait. I was enjoying a noseful by the pier. Then, *BOOM!* A loud noise thundered in the distance, stopping me in my tracks. My good ear twitched. I shuddered.

This time my training said: Get back to Cassie. And my instincts said: Keep sniffing. Training won, and I took off at top speed. I was almost back to where I'd left my girl and her friends when I saw a shiny black car in the distance. I stopped. Watched. My eyes focused down the block and something whizzed by, moving fast. Greyhound fast. So fast I couldn't exactly *see* who it was. But a moment later I could *smell* who it was — the scrawny dogs Cassie'd been trying to rescue.

Training and instincts went at it again. *Get back to your post!* said training. *Follow those dogs!* said instincts. I hesitated, but only for a second. I was a dog, and a dog loved a chase.

The pups tore up the street, weaving. I chased them in and out of alleyways. Buildings. It took all I had just to keep a bead on them. Then I lost them. Just for a minute.

I slowed to a trot. My nose quivered. And I found them again! I took off straight ahead and saw them duck into a burnt-out building.

I sprinted inside after them. I smelled smoke. I screeched to a halt, my paws sliding across the floor. My hackles stood straight up. *Oh! Not here. Oh dog, not here!*

I whimpered as queasiness overtook me. The room whirled. A voice rumbled inside my head. Or outside of it.

*"No, Dodge!"* Mark's voice. Mark? How could it be Mark? Mark was — *"Bad dog!" he shouted*. I whimpered. I couldn't breathe right. I couldn't see. I dropped low, my belly against the cold, grimy floor. I started to back out of the building. I had to get out. But the floor was tilting under my paws. I couldn't walk straight. I couldn't even crawl straight! Then Mark was back. I saw him in my closed eyes. Behind my eyelids.

*"I'm taking this off," he told me. He unstrapped the FIDO. The FIDO was on me, not Hero. He pushed a button on the screen and took out a tiny square of plastic. "To keep you safe. Well, safer." He talked in a hushed tone. "They're coming, boy. But we got here first. And we got what we need. Good boy. You did a good job. Now I need you to stay for a*

*minute, Dodge. Stay!" His voice was serious. Mark disap-*
*peared in the shadows. I whimpered. I stayed.*

I didn't know how long I was in there or where the pups had gone. All I could hear was Mark's voice, calling. Then *ka-boom!* The explosion repeated in my good ear. Over and over. Too many times. I whimpered, confused. What was happening?

My bad ear began to ring, drowning out everything else. I whined pitifully. I wanted to leave this place. Get out. But I couldn't move. Mark had told me to stay. But Mark was dead. My head hurt. Nothing was clear. Nothing made sense.

Something touched my paw. A tongue? Yes, a tongue. I heard a high-pitched bark, from somewhere far away. I opened an eye. It took a long time to focus. A small white shape swam into view. A tiny dog was standing in front of me. Muffet! She'd broken out again. She made a begging sound and licked my cheek. I closed my eyes. She barked. And licked. And barked again. "Yip! Yip! Yip!" She kept yipping.

Then I heard a voice. "Dodge?" It was Cassie. My girl. Her footsteps were fast, running. She dropped to the floor. "Dodge, are you all right?" But she could tell. She could tell I wasn't all right. I licked her hand weakly. More footsteps. Muffet barked and pulled on Cassie's sleeve. "Dodge, we've got to get out of here. I need you to get up."

Cassie grabbed my collar. I tried to walk, but the floor was still tilted. Cassie pulled me behind a burnt-out wall with Muffet. As we dropped out of sight, I saw two figures step into the warehouse.

Riley and Hero.

# CHAPTER 21

I pulled Dodge behind the charred wall, my heart in my throat. I had no idea what was going on with him. He wasn't hurt, but something was wrong — really wrong. I hadn't seen him like this since he first came to live with us. Mom said he was still in shock back then, from the explosion. But what would make him go into shock now?

I inhaled sharply, cutting off my own thoughts, and peered over the low wall we were hiding behind just in time to see Officer Riley and Hero walk into the warehouse. We were hidden from view, thanks to Muffet. Not only did she alert me, she found us a place to take cover.

Could Hero and Riley's presence be making Dodge act so strangely? He was always on guard around them, but . . . I held on to my dog — my poor dog — and hoped they wouldn't notice us.

Peering through a crack in the burnt-out wall, I saw that Officer Riley was dressed in street clothes. That probably meant that he was off duty, but Hero was wearing the FIDO. Again.

"Okay, Hero," Riley said. "Search."

Dodge whimpered slightly, and I held on tighter while Hero sniffed the air. "Rwoof!" He looked our way, and I froze. Hero knew we were here! Luckily Riley didn't understand what Hero was telling him. He just repeated the same command, "Search!"

Next to me, Muffet squirmed. She wasn't wearing her usual figure skating costume. She wasn't even wearing a collar! I put my hand on her back and felt her trembling. All of us were jittery. We had to get out of there before Riley got Hero's message. Only Hero and Riley were blocking the way out, and I wasn't even sure Dodge could make it. He was shaking, and his eyes looked sort of weird and unfocused. Plus he'd barely reacted to Hero's barks. It had to be shock.

Muffet nuzzled Dodge's nose, then grabbed ahold of my sleeve and tugged me backward. I followed, crouching and coaxing Dodge along silently. Muffet walked ahead, looking back at us, and I saw where she was leading — another exit! I moved faster.

For a fleeting second I thought I saw the stray pups hiding behind a pile of rubble. But the dogs, if it *was* them, skulked away and this was no time to go after them. Priority one was to get away from Hero and Riley. Priority two was to figure out what was going on with Dodge.

Outside I took a deep breath but didn't stop. Dodge and I moved like zombies, slow and awkward, but always forward. It took a long time to walk back to my bike, and it was practically dark when my phone beeped, startling me.

**Bittersweet:** R U ok?? Dropping burger thief off at PR with Taylor. I think he likes me ☺☺! Call u when I get home.

**Clued-In:** We r ok. Talk soon.

**Bittersweet:** P.S. I meant the dog, not Taylor!

*Well, that's something*, I thought grimly, staring at my phone.

"Yip! Yip!" Muffet looked up at me with sharp eyes, and I squatted down to thank her for her help. "You really bailed us out of a mess," I told her. Maybe she was paying us back for the Dumpster rescue. Whatever the reason, I was grateful. We might not have made it without her.

Dodge seemed a little more stable now that we were outside and away from Riley and Hero, but he was wiped out. He stuck close to Muffet, who trotted along slowly so they could walk side by side. I got onto my bike and pedaled next to them, keeping an eye on Dodge.

The farther away we got from the creepy warehouse, the more Dodge seemed like himself and the easier I breathed. I just couldn't figure out why Dodge had ended up in that burnt-out building in the first place — or what Officer Riley and Hero were doing there after hours.

As we passed the Happy Produce Dumpster, a hopeless feeling settled over me. I was more confused than ever. Out of the corner of my eye I spotted Mr. Albrici loading crates of cabbages into the back of a truck.

Thinking fast, I patted my pocket. It crinkled, and I smiled to myself. "Hold up, pups," I called out. "We've got a little investigating to do."

Mr. Albrici pretended not to see me as I approached. I knew I annoyed him by bringing around extra dogs, but I wasn't about to give up easily. "Hi there," I greeted. Dodge and Muffet sat down next to me, looking obedient and friendly. "I just wanted to thank you for letting us use your, uh, grabber thingy the other day. So I brought these." I held out the slightly rumpled bag of peanut butter bars. "The bag got a little crinkled," I added sheepishly, "but the bars are from a friend's bakery. They're really good."

Mr. Albrici looked skeptically at the bag, then gestured behind me. "Quite the odd couple, aren't they?"

I turned to look at the dogs. "What? Oh, no, they're not a . . . couple." I stared at Muffet, who was gazing at Dodge adoringly. And even though her haunches were on the ground, her tail was in wagging overdrive. Dodge lay down and let Muffet lick his ear. Holy moly.

*Maybe he's still in shock after all*, I thought wearily. *Either that or this crush stuff is catching.* A picture flashed in my head — Hayley trying to lick Taylor's ear — and I almost laughed out loud.

"Looks like puppy love to me," Mr. Albrici said. "Lots of that going on around here." Then his face clouded. "Of course, I've seen a lot of dog fights, too."

"No kidding," I agreed. "We've actually been in the neighborhood so much because we're trying to bring in some of the strays," I explained. "I work at Pet Rescue."

Mr. Albrici nodded. "Good. The homeless dogs are just adding to the ugly situation down here."

"Ugly?" I echoed, and waited. You'd be surprised what people will tell you if you give them silence to fill.

"Real estate vultures are trying to buy low so they can sell high. I've had this produce business for thirty years! But do they care? No. They're trying to force me out. GreenWay. Ha! *Greed*Way is more like it."

He pulled out a peanut butter bar, bit into it, and chewed furiously. "But I'm not going!" The chewing slowed, and he examined the uneaten portion in his hand. "Say, these are good. Delicious, actually." He popped the rest into his mouth and grinned. "I'd say we're even. . . ."

I beamed. "Even Steven," I agreed, though I was pretty sure I came out ahead, thanks to the tidbit he'd just told me. "And thanks again."

"Yip! Yip!"

"Woof!" Muffet and Dodge barked out their thanks, too, and we were off.

I was hoping Muffet would veer toward home on her own when the time came, but I never got to find out. A couple of blocks from the turnoff, Summer zoomed up to us on her baby-blue bike.

"You!" she screeched as she put on the brakes. "I should have known it was you!" She reminded me of the Wicked Witch of the West nabbing Toto as she snatched up Muffet. "Seriously, Cassie," she snarled. "Dognapping?"

I smiled sweetly at Summer, who held her pup so tightly that Muffet wriggled. "Your dog has excellent taste, Summer."

Summer looked surprised, then beamed. "Of course she does! She's my Muffie!"

"Right," I agreed. "And your Muffie Wuffie has a wittle crush on *my* Dodgie Wodgie!" I cooed, slipping into my normal voice for the punch line. "She's been sneaking out and following him around for days."

Summer's mouth dropped open and she loosened her grip on Muffet, who leaned down to give Dodge a kiss before letting out a happy yap. Dodge licked her back with his giant tongue, and this time I didn't cringe. In fact, I felt a flash of happy satisfaction. "Excellent taste," I confirmed.

"Woof!" Dodge agreed. And we pushed past Summer, heading home.

# CHAPTER 22

I trotted beside Cassie, glad she wasn't pedaling hard. I was tired. Dog tired. And looking forward to home. Bowl. Bed. Bunny. The last couple of hours had delivered some major curveballs — a few I didn't want to think about.

Inside the house not much had changed. Still silent. Still sad. Still filled with the stinging smells of bleach and cleanser and secrets.

I started for the stairs, ready to circle and sleep for a bit. That place. Hero with the camera. Riley and his forced smiles. They made me feel dizzy. Dizzy wasn't a feeling a dog liked to feel.

Cassie was right behind me, but when we walked past The Sister's room, she stopped and looked in. I looked in, too. The Sister was holding scissors. Bits of paper were everywhere. Some of them were stuck to a piece of cardboard on her desk. Some of them were stuck to her. It smelled like glue, The Cat, and really old bread.

"How's the project coming?" Cassie asked.

The Sister shot Cassie a look. If she could've hissed, I think she might have. If she had claws, they'd have been out.

"That good, huh?" Cassie stepped into the room. Slowly. Cautiously. "Need any help?"

The Sister's invisible claws started to retract. She *did* need help. But she'd never ask. Wouldn't say yes, either. She just raised and lowered her shoulders, letting out her breath in a puff.

"Let's see what we've got." Cassie leaned in to study the piece of cardboard. She nodded. She bit her lip. She pulled a piece of paper off The Sister's sleeve. I lay down in the doorway. I didn't understand what they were trying to do. But I could tell it was going to take a while.

# CHAPTER 23

When Sam shot me her death look I almost backed away. But I could tell she was struggling. And not just with her science project, either. With everything. We were all struggling.

Labeled baggies holding moldy slices of bread covered her dresser. Slips of paper with bits of scientific information were on her desk, the bed, the floor, and her arm.

"I hate science!" Sam shouted. She sat down on her bed and ripped the paper scrap — and probably a few hairs — off her arm. "Ow." She pouted, staring at the floor.

"Take it easy. Science isn't that bad," I told her. "I can tell you've done a lot of the work already — you just need to lay it out in a logical order. You know, follow the steps."

Sam's pout stayed, but she looked up at me and stopped complaining. Almost. "I don't even have a title," she muttered.

Dodge lay down in the doorway and heaved a deep sigh. I knew he wanted to be on his bed. It had been a long, difficult afternoon. But Sam needed me.

"You always start with a question, and your question is your title," I explained. "So what's yours?"

Sam looked at me sheepishly. "Does bread mold grow faster at higher temperatures?" she ventured.

"Okay, so write that down."

"It sounds weird."

I nodded. "Science is all about weird and interesting data," I assured her.

Sam blocked out the letters for her title, and then I helped her organize the display. She pretty much had it all ready — including some carefully labeled and impressively blue-green bread slices in baggies. She just needed a little organizing.

"Okay, once you have your question on the board, you

write out your hypothesis — what you thought was going to happen. You've got your process in the data book, and your observations are there, too. Most of your work is done."

Sam stuck her title on the top of the display and looked at me with one side of her face squinched up. "But my hypothesis is wrong," she said.

"No, it isn't." I didn't even know what her hypothesis was, but that was the cool thing about science. It couldn't really be "wrong." "It's okay to disprove your own hypothesis. In fact, that means you learned something. And whatever you learned, that's your conclusion. Get it?"

Nodding, Sam started to write out her hypothesis with a green marker. "Got it," she said, smiling a tiny smile.

"Good." I pushed my hair out of my face and stepped over Dodge. All of that scientific process stuff was making me want to draw some conclusions of my own.

Dodge followed me to our room, circled three times, and lay down heavily on his bed. He didn't even get out Bunny. I sat down on the floor next to him with my notebook. The question I wanted to start with was weighing on my mind, so I scribbled it down.

Question: What has Officer Riley been doing in the warehouse district?
Hypothesis: Riley set Mom up and was planting evidence to make it look like she was responsible for what happened to Uncle Mark.

I paused and chewed on my pen. If my hypothesis was right, the burnt-out building where I found Dodge had to be the one that exploded in the raid. And that made me wonder if Riley was actually trying to do more than make Mom look negligent. Maybe he was trying to frame Mom for Uncle Mark's death because *he* was the one responsible. He definitely had a motive: He wanted Uncle Mark's job. But was he motivated enough to get somebody killed? Was my uncle murdered?

I shuddered. A part of me wanted to believe Uncle Mark's death had been an accident. A part of me *needed* to believe it had been an accident. But what if it wasn't?

When Mom called us for dinner, my stomach was so

tied up in knots there was no way I could eat. Dodge was snoring in his bed and didn't even flinch. I crawled under my own covers with my clothes still on and yelled to Sam that I wasn't feeling well.

I needed to lie there and think. I needed answers. I needed clues. I closed my eyes and saw Riley and Hero in the warehouse. I tried to remember what they were doing there. I was so worried about Dodge I hadn't watched them closely. Replaying it in my mind, I heard Riley yelling commands. And saw Hero with the camera on his head. Suddenly my eyes flew open wide, and I sat up. The FIDO! That was it!

# CHAPTER 24

"Dodge! Dodge!" I woke to Cassie whispering my name. She was leaning over the edge of her bed, her face beside mine. I yawned, letting my tongue curl. My stomach rumbled. Had I missed dinner? I never missed dinner. I loved dinner.

"How do you feel about a trip to the station?" Cassie asked.

*The station?* I hoped she wasn't serious. Was she serious?

"I know. Too much, right?" She'd read my mind. It was all too much. But then her eyes got worried. She threw back her covers. She still had her clothes on. In bed. In the middle of the night. "Don't worry," she told me. "You don't have to go."

Too much for me? Don't have to go? *Woof!* I shook it off. Nothing was too much for me. Where Cassie went, I went. I was a trained K-9. Top of my class. A pro. And Cassie was my girl. I was ready. Ready for anything.

I got out of bed. Together we padded silently down the stairs. The house was silent. Everyone was in their dens. Except The Dad. He was on the couch. I hoped Cassie wouldn't notice and looked back over my shoulder. Was she coming or what?

We slipped outside silently, and Cassie left the front door unlocked.

While Cassie got her bike, I breathed in the night air. It woke me up and made me hungry. It was way past dinner. My stomach growled and I told it to be quiet. We had work to do.

The night was light. There was a full moon and we could see everything. But that meant that everything could see us.

When we arrived at the station we hid across the street and watched. Hero and Riley were just coming out the front doors. Working the late shift. Perfect.

Riley stopped outside the door and set the alarm. We waited until they were gone, then stealthily moved in. Cassie punched in the code fast. I held still, waiting. Then I heard a beep and Cassie pulled the handle. We were in.

I'm not afraid to admit it. Standing in the darkened station after hours made my fur stand up. I started to pant. Just a little. I wanted to bolt. But I would not fail. Not again. Cassie and I had come here for a reason — I just didn't know what it was.

"I want to check something out," Cassie told me as she walked through the cubicles. I didn't like the direction she was heading. My hackles rose higher.

Cassie pushed open the door to Mark's office. *Woof.* I meant Riley's office. I didn't want to go in but couldn't let her go alone.

Inside, the smell of Hero was strong. Irritating. But also familiar. I circled the place. I sniffed Hero's bed, which was exactly where mine used to be, and pawed at it. I wanted to whine, but held it in.

Cassie was over by Riley's desk, looking for something. I didn't know what. I didn't know why we were here. Then

I saw it. Sitting on a shelf. The FIDO. The one Hero had on at the warehouse. Exactly like the one I wore the night Mark died.

I trotted over to it. It smelled like Hero, but that didn't matter. "Whuff!"

Cassie turned. "Oh, there it is!" she whispered, walking over. "Thanks, Dodge."

She sat down in Riley's chair with the screen in her lap. I could hear her heart beating. She pushed a button, and the screen lit up. Hero's recorded bark echoed loudly in Riley's quiet office. "Search!" Riley ordered. His voice sounded a little like Mark's, which put me on edge. I shifted uneasily on my paws. Cassie clutched the FIDO. The light glowed off her face. There was no escaping old memories now.

# CHAPTER 25

I stared at the screen, trying not to let disappointment take over. I was *so* sure that the FIDO would hold a clue, give me information that would make the pieces click into place. I needed them to click into place. I needed to solve this case — for my family to be a family again. Needed it *so* badly! But as far as I could tell, the FIDO contained . . . nothing.

Sighing heavily, I got to my feet to put the contraption back on the shelf. At least I could cross the FIDO off my list of things to investigate. At least I'd confirmed that it was another dead end.

I was just letting go of the camera when Dodge grabbed a strap and tugged it out of my hands. It fell to the floor.

"Dodge, no!" I said sharply. The last thing we needed was to damage police property. I was so drained. And sad. And worried. But Dodge ignored me. He sidled back and barked, nosing the head cam like he wanted to put it on. I looked at him tiredly. "Forget it, Dodge," I said. "We should just get out of here and go home."

"Woof!" Dodge barked again. He picked up the FIDO in his teeth, shaking it lightly in the air. He wasn't giving up.

"You are one stubborn dog," I told him grumpily. "Fine." I strapped the thing on his head and smiled in spite of myself. "Looks pretty good on you, actually," I told him. It suited him more than Hero — sat a little straighter or something.

Dodge trotted to the door and looked at me expectantly. "Dodge, it's not ours," I said. "We've already broken in here; we can't go and steal stuff, too!" I walked up to him, intending to snatch the FIDO off and put it back on the shelf. I wanted to go home. I thought Dodge wanted to go home, too. But when I reached for the camera, he pulled away, stepped back, and gave me a look that said "trust me."

That look made me stop. Dodge was not acting like himself today. The shake-up at the warehouse was weird. But if I trusted anyone in the world, it was Dodge. Plus, it looked like he had a new plan, which I definitely didn't. "We could get in serious trouble for this, you know," I warned.

"Rowf!" He barked his excited bark. He knew, and obviously didn't care.

# CHAPTER 26

My senses were on high alert, and not just because I was worried about getting caught. Because I remembered. I remembered my last night with Mark. I remembered the angry yelling with The Chief. She tried to put Mark in a Sit Stay. She told him not to go anywhere, or do anything. She told him if he disobeyed, she'd fire him. Mark didn't believe it, though. His instincts told him to go. So we went.

When Hayley read The Mom's diary, I listened. I heard all those sad words. I heard the fight. But they didn't make me remember that night. Hearing the FIDO recording did. Hearing Riley give Hero commands in the warehouse. It didn't matter that they weren't the same commands. I remembered. I remembered it all.

*The night was still. No wind. No clouds. A full moon. Silvery light streamed in through the dirty windows, glinting off the warehouse floor. Mark and I were on the case. Mark was my partner. Mark was sure he was right. And his instincts were good.*

*We found the stash of evidence he knew would be there. He whooped and laughed. He showed each piece to the camera mounted on my head. "Capture the memories," he laughed. "Oh, yeah!" He did a victory dance. He wagged his tail. I barked and danced with him while the evidence piled up. "Look at this, Dodge. This proves it! GreenWay is a front for The Corps." He tapped a piece of paper. "And here." He held up another. "This is proof that the city knows!" He pulled documents out of cabinets in the warehouse office. "It's better than I thought!" he crowed. But then it got worse. Much worse.*

*I heard them first. Car motors. Car doors. Unfriendly voices. I smelled onions and lies. Heard heavy boots.*

When I smelled the metal of guns, my hackles rose. My ears twitched. I stood still, listening, while Mark sifted through the evidence.

"What is it, boy?" he asked.

I heard footsteps next. They'd be inside soon. I whuffed low, to let Mark know. He understood.

"They're coming." I saw his body brace. His forehead wrinkled.

"I'm taking this off." He unclipped the FIDO from my head. "To keep you safe. Well, safer." He didn't want them to come after me for the evidence we'd captured. He gave me a pat. He slipped the camera off my head and pushed a button on the screen. The disk compartment popped open. "This oughta do it." He shoved the tiny disc into his pocket and the FIDO into his bag.

Then came the voices. Men — three of them. Maybe four. "They're coming, Dodge. But we got here first. And we got what we need. Good boy. You did a good job. Now I need you to stay for a minute, Dodge. Stay!"

Mark listened near the door. The onion smell got stronger.

*Then Mark disappeared in the shadows. His next command came from the darkness. "Out, Dodge," he said. "Out and stay. I'm right behind you."*

*It was a command — I had to obey. I slunk through the blackness. When I got outside, I was relieved. We'd made it! I turned to Mark. But he wasn't there. I squinted in the dim light. I couldn't see him. My body wanted to move, but moving would draw attention. And the command had been clear. Out and stay. So I sat. I stayed.*

*Then . . . BOOM! WHOOSH! A big explosion rocked the ground, and the warehouse was swallowed by fire. I barked. Mark! Mark was in there!*

*I couldn't stay. I raced inside and was instantly blinded by smoke. I dropped, crawling forward. I couldn't see. Couldn't smell. I fought my way forward. Toward Mark.*

*"Dodge!" the voice choked. "Dodge, it's underneath —" I squinted, coughed, and inched closer. Finally, I reached him on the floor. I grabbed his shirt collar and tugged. He didn't budge.*

*"No, Dodge. No. Bad dog! Get away!" He flapped his arm, shooing me.*

*Bad dog? I reeled. The words stung. My chest felt heavy with shame and confusion. My partner went silent, limp. Soon it would be too late. I had to get out. Had to get us both out. I braced my legs on the floor. I grabbed Mark's pants in my teeth. I pulled as hard as I could. He moved, but only slightly. I felt weak. I braced again, lowering my body to the floor. I leaned back. I pulled. He moved a little.*

*Then, KA-BOOOM! A second explosion rocked the building. The world went silent.*

"Dodge?" Cassie's voice interrupted my memory. We were at the warehouse. I was panting, out of breath. So was she. I didn't know how long I'd been running — remembering. We had to come back here, to the place I wanted to forget. I wasn't going to let it overtake me this time, though. We had work to do.

My bad ear rang as I stared at the warehouse. This was the place where I saw my partner for the last time. After the explosion I went to sleep. Bad sleep. And when I woke up, Mark was dead. Gone. Forever.

"Dodge, why are we here?" Cassie's voice sounded hopeful. And worried.

I went inside, to the place where Mark had lain. To the place where Hero was barking on the tape. The whelp was onto something.

*"It's underneath . . ."*

I got low and started to bark. "Woof!"

I barked loud and sharp. First at one square of floor, then another. It had to be here. It had to!

# CHAPTER 27

I watched Dodge bark at the floor in the burnt-out shell of a building with a lump growing in my stomach. It had been a long day and I had pushed my dog too far. And now he was losing it.

"Dodge," I said softly, hoping to calm him down. I shouldn't have let him put on the FIDO and lead me back here. This was where he'd lost Mark, where he'd freaked out just a couple of hours ago. "Dodge," I called again. He ignored me, moving systematically and barking at the industrial flooring.

The barking freaked me out. It wasn't normal behavior for Dodge, and I worried that it was the start of another episode. Also, it was loud. Broadcasting our presence at night in the warehouse district was *not* a good idea.

"Come on, Dodge," I begged. Hopelessness settled over me. I felt my phone in my pocket and considered calling home. It was so late. I'd be in a world of trouble, but deep down I just wanted my parents to come pick me up. Would it be crazy to call them? I couldn't think straight with Dodge barking.

*What are you doing here?* I asked myself sternly. I regretted going to the station to look at the FIDO at all. We should have stayed in bed. We should have been sleeping.

"Rowf! Rowf! Rowf!"

Dodge's barks were so sharp they made me wince. "Dodge, stop!" I stepped closer, but he backed away from me. "Dodge, no," I pleaded, my eyes tearing. Fear and frustration churned my empty stomach, making me feel sick. This was awful.

Something moved near the wall. I shivered, thinking it was a rat, but caught a glimpse of black and white. The stray pups! I couldn't imagine why they'd come now, with Dodge barking like a maniac. It didn't matter, though. I had no burgers, no crate, no help. If anything, I *needed* help.

"Dodge!" He'd never ignored me before, but he was doing an amazing job of it now. He took another step and kept barking.

"Rowf! Rowf! Rowf!" He stared at the floor like he was standing over a gopher hole. Like there was something in there. I was about to call his name again when I noticed that his bark sounded different — the echo lingered longer in the air. He barked again, louder. And he stopped moving. He looked at me and scratched the floor. "Woof!"

"I hear it," I told him, listening. There was a hollow sound to his bark here, as if there were a space under the tile. I knelt down for a closer look and saw a tiny crack in the floor, shaped like a square.

"Good dog." I gave Dodge a pat, then looked around for something to slide in. I found a piece of slim metal, slid it in, and pried. To my surprise, the sooty square came up easily. I stared into the hole, my mouth hanging open. Beneath it was a fireproof safe!

"So this is what you were trying to tell me!" I glanced at Dodge, whose eyes were locked on the safe. My heart thudded in my chest as I pulled it out, setting the heavy box on my lap. It had a latch and a key slot, and I was sure it was locked. But when I lifted the latch, the safe opened.

My heart felt like it was rising up to my throat as I opened the lid and peered inside, then sank quickly. The safe was empty. Dodge whimpered, and I looked up. "Exactly," I agreed. "Total bummer." But what did I expect? Sighing, I reached in and felt around inside. Nothing. Another dead end.

Dodge lay down next to me, exhaling through his nose. We were both completely wiped out. "We should go home," I said. I was about to close the safe when the moonlight reflected off something secured to the edge. I ran my fingers over it — a small square of plastic, taped to the side near a corner. I pulled it out and peered closer at the tiny square. It was a video memory card. . . . just the right size to fit in a FIDO.

# CHAPTER 28

It was hard not to yip like a puppy when Cassie pulled out the piece of the FIDO. She'd found it! We'd found it! This was the bone that Mark had buried. It was the bone Mark had died for.

I nosed the back of Cassie's hand. I nosed the FIDO screen she was holding, hoping she'd understand. She did. She pushed the plastic into the screen. I heard her press something. There was a click. Cassie stared at the little screen and leaned into me. *Woof.* I couldn't see what she saw, but didn't need to. I'd been there. I'd filmed the piles of paper evidence with my old partner. Papers with pictures. Papers with squiggly lines. Mark held them all up to the camera. If Mark had been a dog, he'd have picked those papers up in his teeth. He'd have shaken them back and forth victoriously. But Mark wasn't a dog. He was a man. A dead man. My tail dropped.

I whimpered, listening to Mark's voice on the recording. *"This is the jackpot, Chief. It's all here. We've got enough to put away Slatterly, the whole core of The Corps, and GreenWay, too! It's one giant mess of sneaky land deals and corruption. Greenbelt, ha! And oh, my. What have we here? Yep. Yep. It's just as we suspected."*

I remembered Mark slapping his leg with the papers. *"Mayor Baudry has been a very naughty boy. Tsk, tsk, Morris. You said you had nothing to do with these guys, but the whole lot of you had your hands in each other's pockets."* My ear twitched. I'd missed that part the first time.

Cassie sucked in her breath. "The Corps. GreenWay. Baudry. They're all connected. . . ." she whispered. "So that means the mayor . . . and Mom." Cassie pressed her lips together. "Oh my God," she whispered in the near dark. "This is huge. And Mom is in serious trouble. . . ."

I whimpered for The Mom. For Mark. For Cassie. And then I heard it — a car door slamming. Right outside the warehouse. I smelled onions. Meatball subs. Metal. I froze as fear seeped under my fur like icy water.

It was happening again.

# CHAPTER 29

By the time I realized what was going on, the mayor and two other men were already inside the warehouse. I should have known when Dodge tensed that he'd heard somebody coming, but I was in shock. Not only had I just been looking at Uncle Mark on a tiny screen, I'd found out what happened the night he died . . . and why.

It was like getting punched in the stomach over and over. The Corps and GreenWay were connected. Mayor Baudry was doing shady business with both of them. And they were responsible for killing Uncle Mark *and* setting up Mom. I was sure of it.

Not only was I in the place where my uncle was killed, I'd just been caught here by the people responsible for it all.

It was too much to take in, so I sprang into action instead. Taking a quick step around Dodge, I blocked the FIDO with my body and held the screen behind my back. I kept an eye on the three men by the entrance and fumbled for tiny buttons. While their eyes adjusted to the near dark, I pressed STOP, FAST-FORWARD, and RECORD. Dodge growled long and low. I knew he couldn't help it, but it drew the mayor's attention.

"Hey, Mayor Baudry. What are you doing down here?" I greeted him first, trying to sound casual and perky. As if we were in a park instead of a burnt-out warehouse. Why not play dumb? If the mayor didn't suspect I was onto him, I might stand a chance.

The three men eyed Dodge and me.

"I thought you said that there was a cop down here, not some girl and her dog," one of the men grumbled. I recognized him immediately: Slatterly.

Baudry silenced him with a hand while I smiled like an idiot. None of them smiled back. It was already clear that my dumb act wasn't going to cut it.

"I could ask you the same question, young lady," the mayor replied. "You and that dog like to snoop, don't you?"

"What? Us? Oh, we were just out for a walk." My smile was starting to feel like a grimace. *Sure we were out for a walk, past midnight, in the warehouse district. . . .*

Dodge was showing his teeth a little. I scooted closer to him, glad he was there. This wasn't some little mess we'd gotten into — it was downright dangerous. My heart was beating faster than the blinking red light on Dodge's FIDO.

"This is Chief Sullivan's daughter. Amanda, isn't it?" Mayor Baudry said, introducing me to his henchmen. He didn't offer their names.

"Cassandra," I corrected. "And this is Dodge, a trained K-9." I swear I saw one of the guys shrink back a little.

Mayor Baudry looked even more annoyed, then started to laugh. "So your mommy sent you to do the job she couldn't, eh?"

I abandoned dumb completely. I put my hand on Dodge's shoulder blades. He was ready to spring if he had to. "You mean the job you won't *let* her do. . . ." I said as

Dodge and I stepped closer. I wanted to make sure the camera captured their faces.

I recognized the bigger guy as I moved in; he'd been with Slatterly outside Happy Produce last Wednesday — the driver. They were both part of The Corps and both wore big black boots. They also looked as though they could squash me and Dodge like bugs. My mind flashed to the strays and their fear of Taylor's footwear. These guys had probably been kicking innocent creatures around the docks for years.

Baudry picked at his teeth, which looked tiny in his big head. "First The Chief sends her brother, and now her daughter. A child. It's pathetic, really." Dodge and I flinched, and Baudry chortled. Then he heaved a sigh, like Dodge and I were an annoying smudge he'd simply have to wipe away. I think he realized that he'd hit a nerve talking about Uncle Mark, though, because he kept going.

"Such a shame to lose a good officer. It happened right here, you know." He made a goofy sad face and my fear turned to fury. Oh, I knew.

"Good officer? I think you mean *great* officer," I said loudly. My voice shook a little but I didn't care.

Baudry stopped talking.

"My Uncle Mark was a great cop. He figured out that you were working with The Corps, that GreenWay was just a cover. That's why he died. You destroyed him along with the evidence that would have sent you to prison." I knew I was walking a dangerous path, that I should probably just keep quiet. But after everything that Baudry had put Mom through, put my family through, I couldn't.

"You're a smart girl, Amanda. You've figured out that your uncle got too close to the truth and died because of it. So tell me, what do you think will happen to you and that dog of yours if *you* get too close to the truth?"

He didn't need to ask — I knew. But anger was giving me courage. Anger, and Dodge. I laced the fingers of my free hand in my dog's scruff. What Baudry *didn't* know was what we had on tape. A shiver snaked up my spine as I braced for the next move. If we were going to take this creep down, I needed a way out for Dodge and me and our evidence.

"I suppose you're feeling rather impressed with yourself. You and your dog there have done a lot of investigating. You're even in the right place. Only your timing is a little off. You see, there's no evidence left. And I can't be seen with these gentlemen. Not by you. And not by that camera." He pointed at the FIDO's blinking light, which clearly hadn't gone unnoticed.

He raised his chin and leveled an angry gaze at me. "Get them!"

Dodge took a step forward. His growl deepened, and suddenly he was in stereo — his growl coming from multiple places at once. No. It was a chorus of growls. The black-and-white strays had crept out of the shadows to flank us. Good dogs.

Baudry and the other men stepped back, afraid of the pack. Very good dogs.

I saw my moment and used it. Sliding my free hand into my pocket, I speed-dialed Mom. I pushed SPEAKER and talked fast and loud. "Mom. It's me. You'll want to record this. . . . I'm here with Morris Baudry and people from The Corps. Kemper, I think. And Slatterly." My hands trembled a little as I blurted out my location. "I'm at the waterfront. In the warehouse where Uncle Mark died."

The men eyed the growling dogs warily, and I knew their fear was the only thing keeping them from grabbing us. That and the fact that they couldn't get all of us at once.

"Stay on the line!" Mom yelled. I heard more noises, maybe a slamming door and a car starting. It was hard to tell.

I wasn't sure how long the dogs and I could hold out. Something would have to tip the scales.

I had no idea it would be Officer Riley and Hero. They burst through the warehouse door in a flurry of uniform and fur. For a second I thought we were sunk — that the police duo was on Baudry's side. Then I saw a flash of metal — Officer Riley's gun. It was trained on the mayor!

"Stop where you are — you're all under arrest!" Riley bellowed.

"Rwoof! Rwoof! Grrr!" Hero echoed.

The three men knew they were caught. They knelt with their hands in the air, and Dodge and Hero circled behind them so they couldn't escape. Riley slapped a pair of handcuffs on the mayor. "You have the right to remain silent. . . ."

"I should have killed that dog when I had the chance," Mayor Baudry spit, glaring at Dodge. Something in his head must have snapped — he didn't seem to realize that everything he said could and would be used against him. Or maybe he figured there was no help for him anymore.

"That dog was with Mark Sullivan last year when we came to burn the evidence. Luckily we had enough explosives to take care of Sullivan. I thought the dog would die with him, but he obviously didn't. And when you kill a cop, someone always has to take a fall."

I listened, stunned. His words came out so easily, like he was talking about the weather. Only he was talking about my uncle. My dog. My family.

Riley continued talking, "Anything you say can and will be used against you . . ."

"Come on, Officer, you have to admit it was genius to make it look like Sullivan's own sister sent him into the mess." Baudry chuckled, looking at me. "Your mother made it so easy. It was like she *wanted* to take the blame. . . ."

I glared at the corrupt creep, glad the FIDO was still recording. He was incriminating himself. But another part of me desperately wanted him to shut up. I didn't want to hear him gloat about killing Uncle Mark and scapegoating Mom.

"That's enough, Baudry," Riley said.

Actually, it was too much. Way too much.

Riley gave me a wan smile. "You're one brave kid. Definitely a Sullivan."

Outside, a pair of cars screeched to a stop. A moment later my parents ran in, followed by Officers Langtree and Walker. I expected Mom to fall right into being chief of police, but she and Dad rushed over to me instead.

"Cassie!" Mom cried, her face full of pain. "Are you okay?" She and Dad wrapped me in a hug, and I shuddered with exhaustion and relief. Tears spilled out of my eyes and streamed down my face. Then Dodge's snout burrowed in, and I put an arm around him, too. We stood together in the place where Uncle Mark had died, hugging one another tightly. We were together, and we were safe.

# CHAPTER 30

"So the cleaning frenzy is over?" Hayley asked. She was on her kitchen floor with Dodge and Hugo — getting a doggie fix — while Alicia and I scarfed peanut butter bars at the counter. We'd come to Hayley's after school to do homework but were ignoring algebra in favor of snacks and relaxing.

I nodded vigorously while I chewed. "Back to regular crazy," I confirmed. It had taken a few days for things to feel okay at 332 Salisbury Drive. "We had a big family meeting with a lot of crying," I explained. "Mom told us that she'd tried to hide what Uncle Mark did — acting against orders — because she wanted him to die with honor. She made it look like she'd ordered the raid with no backup. She's still mad at herself for not searching for the FIDO disk. But the camera was destroyed in the fire and there didn't seem to be enough evidence. She was so worried about Dad she practically did Baudry's cover-up work for him. She even said if it weren't for me and Dodge, Uncle Mark's death could have been in vain." I felt a flash of pride as I told my friends that last part, and Dodge sat up straight and puffed out his chest. He was proud, too.

"Way to go, Dodgeball." Hayley patted him and looked at me with wonder — the way I look at her when she whips up some new chocolate delicacy without a recipe.

"Wow. So what'd your dad say?" Alicia asked, splitting a peanut butter bar into three to share with Hugo and Dodge.

"At first he was a wreck," I admitted. "He thought Mom had been acting guilty because she really was responsible for what happened to Mark. Now that he knows the truth, he's mad at himself for not trusting her. And mad at his brother for acting impulsively. But that was Uncle Mark — impulsive."

"That's intense," Alicia said.

I took a deep breath and let it out. "Right? But at least now that the case is solved and everything is out in the open, we can move on. We can be a family, and Dodge can finally have the couch back." I leaned over and kissed his head. "Oooh, and get this — Mom offered to quit the force!"

Hayley's jaw dropped. "You're kidding."

"Totally serious. My dad almost fainted when she said that — 'cause of course he'd love it if her job weren't so dangerous. But then he said he knew she was a cop when he married her, and he wouldn't want her any other way. After all, Bellport needs a solid police chief, especially when there's a corrupt mayor in city hall!" I rolled my eyes.

"Not anymore," Alicia put in.

The mayor had been removed from office — and not just until further notice — permanently. His trial was pending, but there was no way he'd be back. Ever.

We chewed in silence and were dangerously close to starting our algebra when Hayley's mom came in. She stopped in the doorway and put her hands on her hips, staring at her daughter on the floor with two big dogs.

"What is this, dog central?" she asked.

Hayley sat up, looking a little nervous. She'd told Alicia and me it was okay to bring Hugo and Dodge along, but we all knew her parents were *not* dog people.

"Uh, sorry, Mom. We were just having a little hang time. . . ." Hayley had an arm around each dog, and it was hard to say who was making the biggest goo-goo eyes: Hayley, Hugo, or Dodge.

Mrs. Gault crouched down and gave Hugo a scratch under the chin. "And what are you?" she crooned. "Are you a big bundle of hair and slobber? Yes, you are."

My jaw almost hit the counter, and Hayley and I exchanged looks. For an antidog person, Mrs. Gault had slipped into doggie baby talk really fast. There might be hope yet.

"Let's take these boys for a walk," I suggested, hoping to ignore our homework a little longer. Alicia nodded, we grabbed the leashes, and the five of us scrambled out the door.

"Did you hear that?" I asked the minute we were outside. "She was practically singing to Hugo!"

Hayley's eyes were bright — brighter than when she first met Taylor. "She let him lick her *face*," she added.

I grinned and led the way to Pet Rescue, where a pair of brave black-and-white strays and a certain English bull terrier might be craving a burger and a visit from Bellport's best baker.

We'd only gone a few blocks when I heard a yip that made me cringe and smile all at once. Dodge turned first, and we both spotted Muffet tearing up the sidewalk behind us.

"What is that?" Alicia asked, squinting in Muffet's direction.

"And what is on it?" Hayley added wryly.

Muffet had a pink bow on her head and matching pink booties on three of her feet. We giggled at her outfit as she wagged her way toward Dodge and Hugo.

"That's Muffet, Summer's dog," I told Alicia. Alicia's eyes widened with understanding — no additional explanation necessary.

The three dog tails whipped back and forth like windshield wipers as they sniffed and paraded in circles, taking turns peeing on the same patch of grass. I shook my head, amused. Under the froof, Muffet had the heart of a Saint

Bernard. She'd saved us earlier this week and was growing on me — and Dodge — by the minute.

When the sniffing and peeing was complete, my giant shepherd put out his paws and lowered his head, giving Miss Muffet a full play bow. "Arwoof!" he barked like a puppy. Hugo wandered away to sniff another tree, and the rest of us watched the odd couple and laughed. It was hard not to, and it felt good. In fact, it felt great.

Leave it to Summer to spoil the moment. I leaned down to give Muffet a pat and when I stood back up there was Summer, all huffy and out of breath. She held Muffet's fourth bootie and looked like she'd spent the afternoon sucking on lemons.

"She followed us," I blurted, holding up my hands in innocence. I would *not* be accused of stealing Muffet again.

Summer glared. "I know," she admitted. She blew a puff of air out her nose. "I've been chasing her. Muffet, *come*!"

Muffet ignored her and put her paws up on Dodge's flank, barking. "Yip!"

"Muuuffeeet," Summer whined.

I bit my lips together to keep from laughing while

Summer begged her dog to come. Finally I took pity on her and patted my thigh. Even crushing like a puppy, Dodge was at my side in an instant, looking at my face and waiting for my next word. Our bond was tight and unbreakable. "Good dog," I told him.

Summer quickly snatched Muffet up, and Muffet gave her a loving lick. The little dog acted like she'd just noticed Summer was there and was thrilled to see her. She kissed her again and again until Summer finally smiled.

It was hard to understand, but Muffet obviously loved her owner. They were an odd couple, even in matching outfits.

"Thanks," Summer mumbled to me. I wasn't sure if she was thanking me for putting Dodge on heel so she could catch her dog, or thanking me for bringing Muffet back . . . twice. But I didn't care. She was thanking me and it had to be killing her.

"You're welcome," I enunciated, looking at Dodge. He was back to his old self — feeling better, just like me. He licked my hand and I smiled. Maybe there was a dog out there for everyone.